FACE VALUE
COLLECTED STORIES

PAULA MARGULIES

One People Press
San Diego, California

Face Value: Collected Stories
by Paula Margulies

Cover art by Troy O'Brien.
Author photo by Lisa K. Miller.

ISBN 13: 978-0-9913545-1-1
ISBN 10: 0991354516

One People Press, 8145 Borzoi Way, San Diego, CA 92129
Manufactured in the United States of America

FOR MY FATHER
DOUGLAS DELANO ROCCAFORTE
AUGUST 20, 1935—OCTOBER 14, 2013

With much love

TABLE OF CONTENTS

BIRD SONG

My father sits at the window, a book opened in his lap, his hands resting on the pages. His lips move as if he's whispering, but there is no sound. He wears a plaid flannel shirt, the cuffs and collar frayed, the gray and brown fabric worn soft with age. The shirt is his favorite, one that my mother bought him for his birthday many years ago.

He assumes this position every day, his chair in front of the window facing west toward the canyon. Although he's healthy and active for his seventy-one years, my mother's death has anchored him to his seat. The view is mostly scrub grass and low-lying bushes, but he doesn't seem to see any of it. His eyes stare blankly out beyond the hillsides to the ocean, which is not far from here. His hair is thin, the white and gray strands brushed gently, like long blades of grass, across his scalp. He fingers the pages of his book, a tattered copy of *Don Quixote*, and tilts his head, as if his neck has grown tired. I bring him chamomile tea and a plate of cherries, dark and round, piled like stones.

Eat, Dad.

What? Oh, he says. Yes.

The food goes untouched, and after an hour, I remove the plate and cup and bring them to the kitchen, then return and open the window so that he can enjoy some fresh air. The May breeze feels cool on my face, which is tingly and hot from my morning walk. I often experience hot flashes like this one. At night, I wake from vivid dreams, my body soaked in sweat, my hands shaking. I toss the covers and sit up, take deep breaths, and then wait for the moment to pass. When it does, I shiver and pull the blankets back over me.

Today, the air from the window cools me quickly and carries the sounds of birds twittering as they call to each other outside. I step back and ask if there is anything else he needs.

He looks at me as if I'm a stranger.

No, Elsie. Thank you.

He stares out the window, studying the scenery whose green hues will soon fade into shades of gold and brown.

We live in a two story condo off of Mercy Road in a suburb of San Diego. The building lies close to Highway 15, where cars rush by in a low-level hum. I work at home, typing invoices for physicians. I took this job last year when my mother became ill. For six months she was sick, after finding herself suddenly unable to breathe one day when she climbed the stairs. The fluid in her lungs turned out to be the first sign of an advanced case of cancer. Her doctor ordered chemotherapy and radiation treatments, but the cancer had already spread to her liver. In the end, it settled in her bones, and then wasted no time working its way up her spine and into her brain.

I run my hand across my dad's shoulder and turn to leave the room when I hear a rustling sound. Something small and dark jets past my head, a few inches from my nose. There is a loud thump as the flying object slams into the wall opposite the window.

Oh! my father says. What was that?

My heart is pounding in my chest as I reach for the tiny mass of feathers lying crumpled on the floor below the wall.

It's a bird, Dad. It seems to have knocked itself out.

The bird's body is soft and light in my hand. I check it for injuries, but notice nothing unusual in the faintly streaked brown feathers, the pale white lines on its wings and tail. Its eyes remain closed in tiny slits.

Looks like some type of sparrow, my father says.

He rouses himself from his chair and squints at the bird in my hands, as if examining a specimen in a science lab.

What should I do with it? I ask.

Well, if it didn't break its neck, it'll come to, he says. Maybe you can find a box to put it in.

I cradle the bird in my palm, holding it carefully against my breast as I hurry down the stairs. Peering through the darkness of our attached garage, I locate a box that used to hold some my mother's medical supplies. After dumping small lengths of tubing, gauze pads, and syringes on the garage floor, I place the bird inside. There's plenty of space for air between the top flaps, so I close them and carry it back into the house. I set the box on the kitchen table and take a deep breath. My father comes around the corner, having made his way down the stairs.

What are you going to do when it wakes up? he asks.

I gaze down at the box, the lid closed. There's no movement inside.

Keep it, I say.

Keep it? my father responds. How? We don't have a cage.

I'll go get one. You watch it while I'm gone.

But what if it rouses itself before you come back? His voice trembles.

Just keep the top flaps closed until I come home.

I grab my purse and head out the door.

At the pet store, there's an empty parking spot right in front of the entrance. Inside, the aisles are brightly lit, and the air is thick with the musty smell of vitamins and fur. At the check-out counter, a sales clerk leans forward, leafing through a small catalog. He's tall and thin, with a light spattering of acne across his cheeks and neck.

I'm looking for a bird cage, I say.

Aisle five, on the left, he answers.

I head in the general direction he points and find a number of cages. I've never owned a bird before, but I guess that it would want as much space as possible. I pick out a medium-sized cage, with white food and water cups, and a black plastic bottom with a pull-out tray. After perusing the items on the shelves nearby, I select a bag of seed, then hesitate, uncertain what else I might need. An older man in a red vest appears in the aisle next to me.

Is there anything I can help you with? he asks. His eyes are olive green and his smile is kind.

I'm looking for supplies for a bird.

What type is it?

I'm not sure—it's small and brown. It flew into our house today and took a good thump against the wall. I think it might be injured.

Might be a wren or a house finch, he says. Here's some food that will be good for either one.

He pulls a packet of yellow and red rainbow mix from the shelves, along with a second bag containing thick clusters of tiny brown seeds.

This is millet, he says. Give the bird half a sprig each day.

He hands me a small nest, made of brown twigs and sporting two metal prongs for hanging in the cage, and places a package of a white cuttlebone in my hands.

If your bird doesn't have much coloring, it's probably a female, he says. She'll need the cuttlebone for calcium.

He grabs a couple of short branches with metal hinges on the ends, which he says to place at different heights in the cage to give the bird more roosting spots. After selecting a large bag of bedding pellets, he leads me back to the check-out stand.

This should do it, he says, as he rings the items up. Your bird will want to bathe in its water dish, so be sure to change it every day.

I carry my purchases to the car and rush home in the weak May sunlight. When I walk in the door, I find my father standing in the entryway, one hand holding down the top flaps of the box, a gentle thumping noise coming from inside.

I hold up the cage and dump the bag with the other supplies on the floor.

Quick, dad says, shoving the box toward me. Take it.

How do I get it in the cage? I ask.

I guess you need to catch it.

With my hands? I can hear the incredulity in my own voice. Handling the bird when it was injured was nothing. But the thought of holding a live bird makes me break into a light sweat.

Go on, he says, pushing the box toward me again.

I carry the cage into the kitchen, my father shuffling behind me. I set the cage on the table and pull the door open, then turn and take the box from him.

What if it gets out? How would we catch it?

He seems to consider this for a moment.

Here, he says. He reaches down along the side of the refrigerator and pulls out a paper grocery bag. You open the box and if it flies out, I'll capture it in this bag. He holds the open bag over the top of the box, the paper rustling from the shakiness of his hands.

I set the box on the table next to the cage and slowly lift the edges of the top flaps. The bird cowers in one corner, looking up at me and blinking its tiny eyes. Holding one of the flaps closed, I stick my hand inside and reach for the bird, which thrashes frantically and throws itself from side to side as it eludes my grasp.

Damn it, I say.

My cheeks are hot and flushed, and I can feel moisture breaking out on my back as I reach around and chase the bird with my hand. It flits about wildly, emitting a soft cheeping sound, its wings brushing my hand and wrist as it flutters away from me. My father hovers over us, the grocery bag stretched open in his hands. After a few seconds, I stop and give the bird a moment to settle down. It pauses in one corner, quivering and fluffing its wings at its sides. I make a quick grab for it, and it flies up against my hand. My fingers close and gently trap the tiny body. I can feel the small round head and beak, the soft feathers stroking my skin as it struggles to free itself. The bird's heart beats wildly against my palm.

Look out, Dad, I say.

He drops the bag and steps back, and I shove my entire hand inside the cage and release the bird. It clings to the back bars and then flies madly back and forth before landing on the cage's central perch.

You did it, my father says. His face is stretched in a broad smile.

My mouth is dry, and my hands are shaking. I can still feel the flutter of wings against my palm.

Let's give it some food and water, I say.

Every time I reach inside the cage, the bird panics and throws itself back and forth against the wire mesh. Dad watches as I attach the additional roosts and fill the food and water bowls. I hang the tiny nest in the far right corner and clip the cuttlebone onto one side. My dad opens the millet bag and hands me a sprig. I cut it in half with our kitchen scissors and lay it across the bottom tray.

9

The bird huddles on the center perch, turning its tiny head and watching me out of one eye.

What are you going to call it? my father asks.

I'm not sure, I say. I need some time to get to know it first.

The bird cocks its head as if it's listening, then settles itself, gazing blankly at me through the thin bars of the cage.

Dad takes a seat at the table and watches the bird.

Do you think it will adapt to living in a cage? he asks.

I don't know.

It's kind of plain looking, he adds.

The man at the pet store says it's probably a female.

Not as pretty as the males, are they? He stands up and stretches, then heads back up the stairs, probably to read Cervantes and study the canyon view.

The bird hops about on its perch, keeping one eye trained on me at all times.

Well, I tell it, if you were looking for company, you came to the right place. Not much going on around here except sitting and staring.

The bird flits over to the nest and inspects it for a moment before settling back onto the main perch.

But it wasn't always like this, I whisper.

I can't tell if it's heard me, as it tucks its head under its wing and falls asleep.

In the morning, when I come downstairs, my father is sitting at the table in front of the bird cage.

It's not eating, he says.

The brown bundle of feathers hunkers on the center perch, studying us from eyes like tiny glass beads.

You mean *she's* not eating, I say.

My father looks at me as if he doesn't understand.

It's a female house finch, I explain. I searched it on the Internet.

Well, *she* doesn't like the food.

Maybe she just needs some time to adjust, I say.

We leave the house later that morning. Dad and I cruise along in my Prius to the hospital in La Jolla, where he goes to grief counseling once a week. Today he seems alert, running his hand over his hair and turning to look at me from the passenger's seat.

I don't want to go to this meeting anymore, he says.

Why not?

It's all women there. I don't like being the only man.

I smile at him and try to keep my voice light.

Well, maybe that's a good thing, I say. Maybe one of them will take a shine to you.

When he doesn't respond, twisting his head to gaze out the window, I realize that I've made a mistake. He isn't ready to acknowledge that there could be someone other than my mother in his life.

I'm sorry, Dad, I say. I was only joking.

For a moment he says nothing, then turns to me when we stop at a traffic light.

Do you think it was wrong that we didn't sit Shiva for her?

I glance at him just as the light changes.

Why would it be? I ask. She wasn't the one who was Jewish. I don't think it would have mattered to her.

But still, he says. It doesn't seem right.

He hunches a bit in his seat, wearing his guilt like a tallit.

I reach over and place my hand on his.

It's all right, Dad. We gave her a nice service. It was fine.

My father says nothing.

When we get to the parking structure, I find a spot on the ground floor, pull in, and shut off the ignition. My dad makes no move to get out of his seat.

Do you have any regrets, Elsie? he asks.

What? I'm so surprised by the question, I don't know how to answer it.

Do you have any regrets? he says again. You know, about your life and all?

I listen to the ticking of the car engine, then turn the ignition key just enough to get the air conditioning fan to come on.

You mean about Ryan? I ask.

My father nods.

Yeah, I guess so, I say.

I've always wondered why you didn't say yes, my father says.

It wasn't meant to be, Dad. I glance down at my lap and study my hands.

Why not?

13

I shrug. I don't know, I say. It just wasn't.

I look up at the hospital sidewalk and notice a couple of older ladies, their brown sweaters pulled tight over their shoulders, making their way into the building.

You're going to be late, I say.

I don't want to go, he answers.

Come on; it's only an hour. I'll meet you right here at eleven-thirty.

He reluctantly climbs out of the car and shuffles to the sidewalk. I watch as he takes his time entering the building, moving as slowly as possible to eat up a few of the minutes he has to spend inside.

I reach in the back for a book and step outside. Usually, I buy a croissant and coffee at the food cart in front of the clinic and find a shady spot to wait until my father's meeting is over. But the mention of Ryan has made me restless, so I follow the walkway around the building and out to the wooden steps that lead down to the beach. There is a slight mist on the horizon and the cloud cover, not completely burned off, hangs sullen and gray over the water. I pull off my shoes when I reach the bottom step and let the cool sand caress my feet. Striking out toward the south, where the Scripps pier appears wavy and faint in the distance, I wander along at the water's edge, the chilly surf periodically washing over my ankles. The air is sharp with the smell of salt and rotting seaweed, and the seagulls' cries seem forlorn as they soar above my head.

It was on a beach just like this, near Corfu, that I told Ryan about my mother's cancer.

It was on a beach just like this that Ryan asked me to marry him.

I breathe deeply, taking in the salt air as if it were a steam vaporizer and letting it wash out of me, carrying my sorrow up into the clouds.

Come with me to Morocco, he'd said.

I can't.

Please, Els, he said.

I have to go, I told him. My mother's dying.

I'm dying, he said, pulling me close, cupping my face in his hands. Please, he repeated. Please, please, please. His breath, warm on my cheek, smelled of cinnamon and tobacco.

I pushed him away and walked on ahead of him, my arms wrapped tight around my chest, my feet kicking the white pebbles that coated the shore.

He caught up with me, pulling me to his side.

Stay one more day, he said.

I can't, I answered.

That afternoon, I boarded a bus back to Athens and caught a flight to Rome. He wrote to me a week later and said that he was going to Israel to shoot some photographs for the network. I didn't write back, and though I see his name in the news—in Chiapas, in Afghanistan, in Fallujah—I don't think of him very often. At least, I try not to.

I glance at my watch: eleven fifteen, time to head back and meet my father. I hurry along the shore, splashing through the foamy surf that washes over my feet. The stairs are hard beneath my bare soles, and when I round the corner of the sidewalk toward the clinic, the wet sand feels gritty on the concrete.

Even though it's after eleven-thirty, my father is not yet outside. I buy a croissant at the food cart and find an empty bench, but the pastry doesn't interest me. I pick it apart with my fingers, pulling at the buttery layers as if I'm peeling an onion. When my father emerges from the building, he is walking with an older woman, tiny and gray, a man's beige cardigan hanging from her shoulders. She lifts her face up to his, and he bends his head down to catch something she says. He chuckles, then waves goodbye.

16

When he sees me, he ambles over to my side, then stops and stares at the tattered pieces of dough scattered next to my shoes on the bench.

You're murdering that croissant, he says.

I wasn't hungry, I reply. You want it?

No, he says. Let's go.

I toss the scraps to the ground, and a circle of pigeons quickly forms around us, chuckling and cooing, dipping their gray heads forward as they tussle over the last few crumbs.

My dad hums a tuneless ditty as we head back to the car. I twirl a small feather mindlessly between my fingers, the sand still clinging to my bare feet.

On the drive home, my father is restless, tapping his hands against his thighs, clearing his throat each time he turns to squint out the window.

So, what's her name? I ask.

Who? He turns toward me abruptly, as if I've startled him.

The woman at the meeting. The one you were walking with.

Oh, that's Elizabeth Hansen, he says. A brief smile flits across his lips.

Is she nice? I ask.

Oh, yes, yes, very nice, he says. He pauses a moment. I think our conversation is finished, but then he says, She's a card player. Bridge.

Ah, I say. You used to like that game.

Yeah. He runs his hand over his head. Not as much as I like cribbage and backgammon, but I was good at bridge, I suppose.

We say nothing as I ease the car into the driveway and wait for the garage door to swing upward.

I follow my dad into the house and find him standing before the bird cage. He says nothing for a moment, then turns toward me.

I'm sorry, Else.

For what? I ask.

He moves aside, so I can see the cage. The bird lies crumpled in the corner, its eyes closed, its tiny feet curled up against its body.

Oh! I bring my hand to my mouth, feeling first the tingly spread of heat across my back and shoulders, and then a chill as my skin begins to sweat.

I guess it didn't like being cooped up, dad says.

I pat his arm, and then wipe a tear from the corner of my eye.

I'll take care of it, I say.

I spend the next twenty minutes rummaging through the garage until I find a box small enough to act as a coffin for the tiny bird. I bring it inside, along with a shovel and some tissue paper from the hall closet.

When I remove the bird from the cage, its wings are smooth and cold in my hand, its feet and head almost weightless against my palm. I lay the tiny body in some tissue paper inside the box.

My dad watches from his kitchen chair.

Where are you going to bury it? He asks.

Under the rose bushes in back, I say.

I gather the box and the shovel, and as I turn to go, the telephone rings.

I'll get it, dad says.

I hear him say hello as I head for the back door, and then I hear something I haven't heard in a long time. He chuckles, and then laughs out loud.

Why, yes, I think I could be a fourth on Sunday, I hear him murmur, his voice soft and friendly.

I push the back door open with my elbow and stumble along the cement walkway to my mother's garden, where a few of her favorite Sterling Silver roses, their branches shaggy and in need of pruning, lift their faces to the sun. As I push the shovel into the hard California clay, I can hear my father's voice murmuring yes, yes, as if he's listening to someone give directions.

When I finally have a hole big enough, I set the box inside the tiny grave and smooth the dirt with my hands. As I pack the dirt on top, I watch my own hands press down on the dry soil, the pale skin and long tapered fingers reminding me of my mother's hands as they lay against the blanket, so still and helpless in her hospital bed.

I rub my palms together to shake off the dirt and wipe them against my jeans, and study the soft mound of dirt before me. The birds twitter noisily in the carrotwood tree on the other side of the yard, and near the rose bed a group of mourning doves pecks at the seed scattered below the feeders that hang from its branches. Inside the house, I can hear my father signing off.

Yes, yes, all right. Well, I'll see you then. Goodbye.

Yes, goodbye, I whisper. My heart flutters in my chest.

I gaze down at the small grave at the foot of the rose bushes and feel my eyes well up with tears. I let them run down my cheeks, as I stare at the overturned dirt before me.

I cry for my mother, for the long sad months of waiting as her body raged against the cancer that destroyed her.

I cry for Ryan, for the love that I used to feel for him.

I cry for my father.

I cry for the tiny creature that lies beneath the dry earth at my feet.

I cry for myself.

When I can't cry any more, I wipe the tears from my face, and rub my nose on the edge of my sleeve.

I pick up my shovel, and just before I turn to go a hummingbird zooms past my head, its tiny body hovering in front of me, its bright green feathers shimmering in the light. It hovers before me, so close I can hear the electric thrum of its tiny wings. It stays there for just an instant, its buzzing echo loud in my ears, before zooming off into the afternoon sunshine.

As I near the back door, I hear the telephone ring again.

This time, I wonder if it will be for me.

OBEDIENCE TRAINING

If I'd known the dog had rabies, I wouldn't have petted it. I would have kicked it, or chucked something at it, or even better, walked away.

I was sitting at the park next to my building at work, eating my lunchtime tuna sandwich, when the dog first appeared, nosing around the brown bag at my feet. It was one of those ratty looking terrier-types, with a coat like a matted-down bathroom rug. I said, "Hey there, buddy," and reached out to pat its head. That's when the fucker bit me. Hard. After a trip to Urgent Care that left me two hundred dollars poorer, I returned to work with a vial of antibiotics and a bandage on my left hand.

My coworker, Mildred, eyed the white gauze.

"What did you do to yourself, Carolyn?"

"Dog bite." As I stepped into my cubicle, I noticed two of the secretaries huddled together near the entrance to the copy room.

"I heard he was cheating on her."

"Didn't she catch them in her own bed at home?" The exaggerated stage whispers could be heard across the room.

When I approached, they reared back like startled snakes, guilt pulling at their faces.

"Actually," I said, "it turns out that Mark is gay. I hear he's been sleeping with both of your husbands."

I headed for the women's room. After slamming shut the door of the largest stall, I slid to the floor and leaned my cheek against the cool, tiled wall. Which was worse: having to end a marriage that I'd considered whole and beautiful, or having its demise be so public?

I fingered the gauze bandage on my left hand, already beginning to turn gray along the edges. While I peeled the bandage away to examine the wound, I remembered the time Mark had told me that he didn't want to be married anymore.

"Why not?" I had asked, stunned at this revelation from the man who was my best friend.

"Because you haven't been happy these past two years," he'd answered. "I guess I haven't been either." Wincing at the recollection of these words, I stared at the dark red holes that the dog's teeth had left in my hand. They were angry-looking welts, and they wept a little as I pressed the skin around them with my thumb.

When I got back to my desk, there was a Post It™ note stuck to my computer screen, with a message that Animal Control had called. They had caught the dog that bit me and put it down. I felt a little sorry for the dog; it couldn't help the fact that it was sick. As I crumpled the note, my desk phone rang. I froze when I heard the voice that answered my hello.

"What do you want, Mark?" I tried to keep my tone steady.

"I miss you," he said.

With those words, the dog at the park flashed into my mind, only in my mental image it was sitting patiently before me, its warm brown eyes moist and tender.

"Carolyn, are you there?" Mark's voice had an urgency to it that I hadn't heard in a long time. "Can you meet me tonight? I want to see you."

I held up my bandaged hand and flexed it, feeling the soreness as my fingers curled together. Would I? Should I? I squeezed the receiver with my good hand.

24

"No." The word floated from my mouth as if in a bubble and hung in the air, forbidding and huge. I dropped my bandaged hand and let it dangle at my side. Outside the window near my cubicle, I could see the park, lush and sparkling in the sunlight after a light sprinkle of rain.

On a curving pathway, a small woman walked a golden retriever. The animal trotted obediently in smooth, bouncing steps on the end of the leash its owner had wrapped around her hand.

FACE VALUE

I push back the curtain from the living room window and rest my cheek against the glass. The cold windowpane sends a chill through my skin and down to my neck and arms. Outside, the world is black, the trees backlit in a soft, hazy glow. There is no wind, and no one stirs in my neighborhood. The Franks are not arguing, the Echols kid does not do his clattering dance on his skateboard, the Gibbons' dog must be asleep because I don't hear its deep, repetitive bark. All is silent, cold and still, like the marble on a tombstone or a good piece of dark, green jade in the palm of your hand.

If I lean back from the window, I can see my own reflection in the glass, ghostly and pale, the dark outline of a middle-aged woman. Around me are my flowers, my books, and my drawings. With bits of charcoal and tissue-thin sheets of onion paper, I create pictures of faces: the faces I see in my dreams, the faces I see from my window, the faces I know from my past. I tape them to the walls and they watch over me, mute witnesses to the small daily rituals that take place in these rooms.

I've lived in this house all my life. I don't go out any more, because I don't have to. A checkout clerk at Ralph's delivers my groceries. My Aunt Tina purchases clothes for me, or I order them online. I've a car, but it has not left the garage, where it's parked, for ten years. I don't water or trim my lawn; a Mexican man named Angel comes once a week and mows the grass and pulls what few weeds stand out along the curb. When the maple tree in my front yard loses its leaves in the fall, I don't rake them. I prefer to watch them scatter in the warm Santa Ana winds that blow in from the desert. Later, when the rains finally come, I lay awake at night and picture them decomposing, wet and matted down.

I used to see a doctor for my condition, when my parents lived here with me. The doctor prescribed small blue pills to take twice a day, and I took them for two years. Those were the years after high school, when I went to college and worked at a daycare center. I drove away at 8:00 a.m. five days a week and returned in the evening, after my classes were over. On the weekends, I studied or helped my mother cook or ironed my father's shirts. In the evenings, I watched television before I went to bed.

My world seemed to be the same, over and over, day after day. Then, one morning, while driving the freeway on my way to work, I felt light-headed and dizzy, and sure that my heart was about to stop. I took the nearest exit and piloted the car back home, gripping the steering wheel. After driving the car's front wheels over the curb in front of my house, I staggered to my bedroom, sweaty and shaky, and slept the rest of the day.

Two days later, when approaching the freeway on my morning commute, my head exploded with lights. Heart racing, I steered the car back to my house, never to venture out again on my own. I stayed in bed for the next five days, until my mother dressed me and took me back to the doctor. He told me he could make me feel better and that I had to keep taking the pills. But I knew that what he said wasn't true. There is no cure for wanting to be alone.

Of course, you're never alone when you're surrounded by your family. The Italian relatives on my mother's side say that family is everything. *"La familia!"* they exclaim, as they raise their glasses of Chianti. *"La familia!"* they cry, when a family member is hurt or, worse, dies. "*La familia*!" they lament when someone commits the greatest crime of all, which is to leave the family behind. My uncle, Johnny, did that, and the family never forgave him. I forgave him, but I had nothing to lose by doing so. I had everything to gain from knowing that he would never come back.

My mother wept openly when Johnny refused to return her phone calls and, finally, disappeared altogether.

"My baby brother," she cried. "How could he do this to us? How could he turn his back on the family?" Through the walls in my bedroom I could hear her muffled voice, alternately angry and whimpering, as she unloaded her frustration and guilt onto my father.

"Carmella," my father said, "we've done everything we can for Johnny. We gave him money, we bailed him out of jail, Christ, we even let him live here for a while. There's nothing more we can do for him. Let him go."

"But why, why?" she wailed.

I knew why he left. She did, too, although she would never admit it. Johnny left because he could. He left because he knew that there was nothing to tie him here. He left because of me.

But that was a long time ago. Now, as I stand at my window, I am truly alone and while it is always quiet, there is no emptiness in my life. My world is filled with the small moments of making a day, of choosing my clothes, of deciding what kind of tea to make in the morning, of watering my violets, and fingering the smooth velvet on their wide, green leaves. I can turn on the television set if I want to, or surf the Internet, but I find that most of my day is spent watching the neighborhood through my front window and drawing pictures of the faces I see there.

My favorite neighbors to watch are the Franks. They are a middle-aged couple, in their late fifties, with two sons who have grown and moved away. I used to babysit their sons when I was in high school, but I don't see them come around anymore. Emma Frank was once thin and pretty, a small active woman who loved to play tennis and garden in her backyard. She hasn't come out of her house carrying her tennis racket in a long time, and lately her yard is weedy and overgrown with crabgrass. Her gray hair hangs limp around her face, and she wears long, dark knitted sweaters and baggy jeans, even in the summer.

I see her in the late mornings, walking slowly away from her front door with a puzzled expression on her face, as if she's forgotten something, or can't remember where she's supposed to be going. She often carries plastic shopping bags of fabric, with bits of cloth and thread falling out onto the sidewalk. When they fall, she hastens after them, like a mother hen trying to recapture her children.

I watch her husband, Henry, leave for work every morning at 6:00, wearing his dark blue windbreaker and carrying a thermos and an old, battered brown briefcase. He sets the silver thermos on the roof of his car and throws his briefcase into the front seat with a sharp flinging motion before he drives off. Once, I saw him leave with the thermos on top of his car, but I didn't run out to tell him. I wanted to see if it would fall, or if he would stop, having realized it was still up there, but he never did. He just drove down the street, his thermos sitting erect and tall on the roof, like a flag post leading the way on the early morning commute.

The Franks fight constantly and, though I can't make out what they're saying, I can hear wisps of angry words and dull, bumping noises echoing from across the street, like a telephone connection that isn't quite clear. Once, after one of their fights, Henry burst out the front door, his jacket in his hand, and slammed the door of his car before careening off down the street. He didn't come back until the next day. Emma left the house with swollen, red-rimmed eyes and balls of Kleenex in her hand and walked the neighborhood, circling our block five, ten, maybe fifteen times that afternoon.

My parents used to fight like the Franks, and most of the time the arguments were about family. Before Johnny came to live with us, my parents argued about him continuously.

"But, Dominic, he's my brother," my mother cried one night. "So he's made some mistakes. What's wrong with helping him out a little? He would do the same for you if you were in his shoes."

"Johnny wouldn't help anyone, Carmella, and you know it," my father said in his calm, quiet voice. "He's a loser. He doesn't care about anyone but himself."

"How can you talk that way about my brother? He's my blood!"

"He's no good, and I don't want him around Francie."

Of course, my father lost this battle, as he did all the battles he fought with my mother, and my uncle Johnny came to live with us when I was fifteen years old. He stayed for one year, and that year was filled with mystery and wonder and, later, with the bitter aura of regret.

A few weeks ago, when I looked out my window, I noticed that my neighbor, Emma, had a visitor. A tall, heavyset man, with silvery hair and a wide rear end stood on her porch, hands in his pockets, looking first left and then right until Emma answered the door. When she finally appeared, her face broke out in smiles, and she touched the man's arm as she pulled him into the house. I stood and fingered the collar on my flannel shirt, remembering when Johnny had come to live with us and I had touched his arm the same way.

"See this, Francie?" Johnny had said, pointing to his flexed bicep, his elbow braced against the worn gray Formica on our kitchen table. "This is pure steel. Go ahead, feel it."

It was a weekday afternoon after school, and my mother had gone to the butcher to buy some pork to make sausage. Johnny had just come to stay with us and I was fascinated by his long dark hair, slicked back from his forehead; the packs of cigarettes and stacks of automobile magazines he kept on the nightstand next to his bed in our spare room; the cool way he tilted his head back when he drank beer with my father at the end of the day. Sitting across the kitchen table from him, I felt in awe of his maleness and his hip, older attitude. I was afraid to touch him and, at the same time, wanted to more than anything.

"Go, ahead, Francie. See if you can bend my arm down."

I glanced at his face to see if it was truly all right, but he wasn't looking at me. He was staring at his own arm, a pleased, childish look on his face. I slowly reached out my hand, and placed my forefinger on his bicep, lightly, as if I were going to tickle him, or brush something away. I slid it down his arm, all the while staring at his face, daring him to break his concentration on his own arm, daring him to look at me. But he didn't move at all, watching intently as I traced my finger carefully toward his wrist. We both held our breaths, and when my finger reached the base of his hand, he curled his fingers around it tightly, and finally looked up at me, a lopsided smile on his face.

"Gotcha," he said.

But I had him. From that moment on, Johnny was mine, a personal prize, a family member caught in my spell, controlled by me.

I drew nothing but Johnny that year. Pictures of Johnny sitting in the armchair in our living room,

Johnny behind the wheel of his car, Johnny waiting for me outside my school, Johnny behind my bedroom door. Once, we lay at the foot of one of the oak trees in the park and I placed a stack of pictures on his chest.

"I drew these for you," I said.

Johnny lifted the stack from his chest and bent his head forward to look at it. A light breeze blew the thin sheets over his hand, and he had to flip them back to see them.

"They're great, Francie. Terrific."

He laid them on the ground next to us without having looked past the first one, and turned toward me, his eyes at half-mast, a lazy smile on his face.

"All you do is draw," he said. "Can't you do anything else?"

I picked up the first picture and held it in my hand and then glanced up at Johnny. Without taking my eyes from his face, I tore it in half, and then in half again, and then a third time. I took each sheet and tore it the same way, until there was a pile of jagged white pieces on the grass between us.

"Yeah, I can do something else," I said. As I leaned forward to kiss him, the warm midday breezes lifted the bits of paper around us and scattered them like giant flakes of falling snow.

My mother was waiting for us when we got home. She stood at the stove, her gray-streaked hair in a tight knot at the back of her head, one hand on her hip, the other stirring peppers and onions in a pan of sizzling oil.

"Where have you been?" she said, looking first at her brother and then at me.

Johnny walked over to the refrigerator and pulled out a beer.

"We went for a walk," he answered, raising an eyebrow at me as he strolled over to my mother and put his arm around her waist.

"That smells great, Carmella. Just like mama used to make."

My mother didn't answer him as he kissed her lightly on the forehead and left the kitchen. I had my hands in the pockets of my skirt and, with my head down, tried to follow him, but my mother stepped in front of me.

"I know what's going on," she said, waving her wooden spoon in my face. "I won't have it, Francie. Not in my house. Do you hear me? Not in my house." She accentuated the beat of the last four words with wild swings of her spoon.

"I don't care what you think!" My hands shook and my cheeks burned, but the words sprang forth, like hungry dogs. I turned them loose, let them off their leashes, let them leap forward into my mother's face. "You're just jealous because you want Johnny, too." My mother's face contorted, her mouth opening and her eyes filling with tears. I pushed past her, shoving her into the stove, and racing out of the kitchen and up the stairs to my room.

I had never stood up to my mother before. I had always been her dress-up doll, her unwilling confidant, her greatest sacrifice, her punching bag. While she preened and fake-smiled at the neighbors, my teachers, and the people at church, I heard her cursing them as she chopped parsley for meatballs, heard her laugh when one of them suffered some mishap, and listened to her berate my father and me for ever thinking that anyone outside our family was any good. My uncle was the only person she never criticized, never tortured, never hurt. I watched her fawn over Johnny in a way that she never fawned over me, and I knew he was the only person who truly held a place in her heart.

That day, though, I couldn't see her, couldn't hear her voice. All I saw was Johnny's face, and the fact that he was mine. I threw myself on my bed and sobbed into my pillow, wondering if Johnny would sneak in to comfort me or commiserate, to plan some wicked escape. But when I finally went to his room to look for him, Johnny was nowhere to be found. He did not come home for dinner, and the next morning, he was gone.

He left nothing in his room but one of my drawings on his pillow. It was one I had done about a month after he came to live with us, showing Johnny asleep in his bed, his left arm back, curled behind his head. His eyes are closed and there is a hint of a smile on his face, as if he is lost in some wonderful, peaceful dream. I keep that picture on my nightstand, next to my bed, and imagine that Johnny is watching over me when I go to sleep at night. When I close my eyes, I dream about the two of us walking hand in hand through drifts of delicate white snowflakes. I wake each morning surrounded by sheets of drawings, my arms curled tightly around my pillow.

The other day I sat at my living room window and watched my neighbor, Tim Evans, put up a basketball hoop for his youngest boy, Todd. Tim's head was bent above his son's, the two of them with matching mops of curly blond hair, joined together in total concentration as they hammered and pounded and stopped to read the sheet of directions that kept threatening to blow away down the street. I sketched the two of them in silhouette, Todd's face overlapping his father's, and watched as they worked together, a pair of suburban soldiers erecting a monument to domestic life.

My own father had never been good with hands-on projects. Although he was artistic and well known for his technical drawings in the aerospace industry, he wasn't able to translate that ability to anything tangible. When I was ten years old, I remember he built a hutch for my two pet rabbits, Snowflake and Peter. I can still recall the look of utter dismay when the door wouldn't latch properly on the first try.

"Well, look at that, Francie," he had said. "Not the best fit there, eh?"

My mother had shaken her head, arms crossed, when she saw the too-short latch, and the gap between the door and the rest of the cage.

"Those two rabbits will be eaten by coyotes if they have to count on you for shelter," she said.

The rabbits lasted two years before they finally did escape, when I inadvertently left the door open after feeding them one morning. Even so, the look of surprise on my father's face whenever he realized that something wouldn't work became his standard expression. He had the same look on his face the last day I saw him. Tubes were running from him in every direction and he was so weak it was an effort to open his eyes when I walked into the room.

"Francesca," he said. "The button doesn't work. I press it and press it and no one answers."

"Let me try, dad," I said, and watched as the orange-yellow attendants' light flashed the moment I touched the button.

"Will you look at that," my dad said, a momentary flash of awe flitting across his face, bringing back the days of my childhood so vividly I had to turn away to hide my tears.

My mother had driven me to the hospital that morning. On the way home, I stared out the window, wondering how life would be without dad's gentle humor, his recurring absentmindedness. My mother had badgered me for weeks to get out of the house and visit him, but my inability to drive had me in its grip, and I only saw him that one time. The next time was at his funeral. It was the last time I ever went anywhere in a car.

My mother passed away shortly after my father died, and her sister, my Aunt Tina, took care of me during the weeks before and after the funeral.

"All these pictures, Francie," she said, lifting pages of thin white sheets off the dining room table. Small and bird-like, with a tight bun at the back of her head exactly like my mother's, Aunt Tina bustled about the room, shoving papers into a neat pile. "You need to put these somewhere, so they're not in the way."

I lifted my head from my arms, drowsy and blurry-eyed, and looked at her without speaking. It had been one week since I had found my mother's body on the bathroom floor, lying crumpled like a broken doll. As I watched my aunt move briskly around the room, I thought of my mother, standing at my father's funeral with one hand on his casket, her head bent below her black veil as tears dripped on the novena card that quivered in her other hand. That memory seemed to grow until it enveloped me, and I began to shake.

"Francesca, what's wrong?" Aunt Tina asked. She hurried to my side and wrapped her arms around my shoulders. "You're trembling so hard. There, there. There, there." She rocked me gently, and in the rush of heat from her hands I felt the years of anguish and pain well up into deep, heaving sobs that I could not control.

"It's going to be alright," my aunt crooned. "Your parents left some money for you, and I'll help you. You won't be alone, Francesca, I promise."

Aunt Tina kept her promise, and during the past five years she and her husband, Uncle Gio, have come to the house on and off to bring me clothes and groceries and to see if they could help with any household repairs. But they are older now and it's getting hard for them to visit. Uncle Gio's diabetes causes so much numbness in his feet that he can no longer drive, and Auntie T's cataracts have affected her sight so she has difficulty seeing.

During one of her visits one evening, while we shared glasses of anisette in my living room, she placed her hand on the couch cushion and pulled at the corner of it.

"There's something here, Francesca."

She pulled the piece of paper out from under the cushion and held it, creased and wrinkled, in front of her.

"Why, it's a baby. It looks like your father." She held the drawing at arm's length, peering down at it through her bifocals. "This must be one you drew from Dominic's photo album."

I took the drawing from her and held it in my lap, caressing the edges. While my aunt droned on about the private lives of various family members, I gazed at the infant's tiny head, its small chubby hand nestled below its cheek. I ran my finger over and over the fine hair on its neck, until the charcoal started to smudge and blur.

"You know, when we were growing up, we had it hard, Carmella, Johnny, and I. Our parents didn't have a lot of money and times were difficult for our family. And I know that Carmella babied Johnny, we all did. But, Francesca, she always loved you." Aunt Tina stopped to peer at me closely, her eyes large and cloudy behind her glasses. "I know she had difficulty showing it, but you were her whole world, her whole life."

I gripped the drawing tightly in my lap and breathed slowly and evenly, trying to keep calm, fighting back tears.

"Whatever secrets you have, Francesca, your mother shared them with you." Aunt Tina reached over and placed her hand over mine, on top of the baby's charcoal image.

"Thank, you, Auntie," I said. I kissed her on the forehead. Later, I hugged her especially hard before she went out the door, the drawing clutched in my hand. After she left, I closed the door and slumped to the floor, wrapping my arms tightly around my shoulders, the child's image pressed against my breast.

After Johnny left, and I got morning sickness, my mother had taken me to the doctor's. She never told my father, I suppose, because she couldn't bear to have him think badly of her brother. Perhaps she expected me to have Johnny's baby in the hopes that it would somehow fill the void that he had left in her life.

But I didn't have the baby. I slipped away in my father's car on a late summer evening to a clinic downtown, and left cramping and bleeding and vowing to never let anyone leave me behind again. When I told my mother that I had lost the baby, she became silent and withdrawn, and the two of us moved about the house like cloistered nuns, pensive and brimming with unspoken words.

Since I had used all the money I had saved from babysitting and relatives' gifts to pay the clinic, and I had nowhere to go, I stayed with my parents and watched each year slip away, like another sheet torn off my pad of drawing paper. My college teachers praised my drawing talent, and one of them tried to get me to enter a special school for the arts, but I found myself moving farther and farther away from the outside world, until I couldn't bear to even drive a car.

And, so, I find myself at my window, watching my neighbors go about their lives and greet the world that comes to their doorsteps. Sometimes people come to my door, too. Yesterday, a man rang the doorbell and when I answered, he asked if he could use my telephone, because his cell phone wasn't working. I lied and told him no, that the phone was disconnected. He smiled, a really nice smile I thought, and thanked me anyway. I have seen him before because he comes to read the electrical meter on the side of our house. I always know when he's coming, because he whistles show tunes, like *Oh, What a Beautiful Mornin'* from *Oklahoma!* or the theme song from *Cabaret*.

I've watched him through my window, taking his lunch break in his white pickup truck. In the summer, he likes to park his truck in the shade under my maple tree. He usually eats a sandwich and reads a book, and sometimes he talks on his cell phone. I see him lean his head back when he talks, and sometimes he laughs into the phone. He looks a little like the actor who played Opie on *Mayberry RFD*, with straight blond hair and freckles and a turned up nose that looks strangely childlike on a man.

The next time he comes to the door, I might talk to him. I might even let him inside.

FREE FALL

Sixty-five-year-old Irv Kaplan awoke one September morning and decided that he had no life.

He sat up in bed in his worn striped flannels, looked at the tiny blue veins lining the tops of his pale feet, and thought, I am no one. Today I will discover who I am or I will not live anymore.

Heaving his saggy body out of bed, Irv stumbled to the bathroom of his Los Angeles apartment. The light above the mirror buzzed wearily and Irv winced at his reflection in the gray-green glow. Reaching for his razor blade and shaving cream, he noticed the liver-colored spots on his hands and the way his fingers trembled, as if directing a silent symphony. He shaved slowly and solemnly, smelling the lemony scent of the shaving cream, feeling the dull razor skip as it scraped roughly over his chin and across the tender underside of his neck. When he finished shaving, he watched the foam, speckled with gray hair, swirl around the stopper before spilling over the edge of the drain.

Irv combed through the shirts in his closet until he found his favorite, a plaid cotton with short sleeves. He put on khaki pants, carefully tightened his belt, tied his shoes, and set a small green gym bag on the bed. Inside it he placed his wallet, his LA Dodgers windbreaker, and *Street & Smith's 2001 Guide to Baseball*. Pausing a moment, he listened carefully to the sounds of his wife in the kitchen downstairs. He then slid the gym bag's zipper closed and headed down the stairs.

In the kitchen, his wife Rose sat at the pinewood table, her white hair a lion's fringe above her head, her breasts pendulous and creamy under her thin nightgown. She held the paper at arm's length in front of her with one hand, while the other gripped a Caesar's Palace coffee mug.

"Bad news for the market yesterday," she said, not lifting her eyes from the page. Irv placed a slice of Jewish rye in the toaster and stood over it, listening to the hum of the coils and the snap of the popping seeds. After spreading a small bit of margarine on his toast, he wrapped it in a paper napkin. Before picking up his gym bag, he stepped toward his wife and kissed her gently on the forehead. Then Irv took his bag and his toast and, for the last time, walked out his apartment door.

The morning air was cool on Irv's cheeks as he stood at the foot of the steps outside his building. He wasn't sure which way to turn at first, and then decided to head for the bus station a few blocks to the left. His gym bag bumped his leg as he walked, and the toast felt warm in its napkin, like a miniature heating pad. As Irv strode forward, he recognized the sounds of the birds in the bare-branched jacaranda trees that lined the block. There was the insistent cooing of the mourning doves, the twittering chirps of the sparrows, the raucous caws of the bullying crows. The street seemed alive to him this morning, and Irv decided that was a good thing because inside he felt silent and empty. He had been that way for a long time; in fact, he couldn't remember feeling differently, although he knew that at some time in his life he must have experienced great joy.

At the bus station, Irv stood under the day's schedule and gazed up at the list of destinations. Santa Ana, Irvine, Mission Viejo, San Diego to the south; Pasadena, Glendale, Santa Clarita, Ventura to the north. Irv couldn't decide where he wanted to go, so he turned to the seating area across from the ticket window and sat down in the only open space. On his left, an elderly woman, her wispy white hair barely covering the tender pink of her scalp, nodded over a tattered Bible that trembled in her shaking hands.

To his right, slumped in her seat with CD headphones strapped across her hair, a young Latina rocked her head to the barely audible thumps of rap music, arms wrapped tightly across her chest. Irv noticed that her nails were bitten to the quick and her denim jeans had the dull sheen caused by too much dirt and wear. After carefully setting his gym bag between his feet, Irv unwrapped his toast and tore off half of it.

"If you haven't had breakfast yet, you're welcome to share mine." The girl looked at him defiantly before sliding the headphones toward the back of her head. Her nostrils flared slightly, showing a small pierced hole on the right side where a stud must have sat at one time.

"I don't need no food, old man, so leave me alone." Her hair and body bristled with anger, but her eyes were dead and tired. When Irv looked into them he was startled by a sudden shock of recognition.

"I'm sorry. I didn't mean to disturb you." Irv studied the piece of bread in his hand and then took a bite of it, chewing thoughtfully and trying not to make eye contact with the young woman next to him. As he reached into his gym bag to pull out his *Street & Smith's*, he noticed the girl's feet. Her black canvas tennis shoes had turned brown, caked with dirt and mud, and the sole was separated from the upper portion of the shoe on her right foot. On the floor next to her seat was a black vinyl bag, also stained and torn, stuffed with a sweatshirt, bundled up clothing, and a brown paper bag. This girl is a runaway, Irv thought to himself, and he looked up at her again only to catch her staring openly at him. She held his gaze, steadily, without flinching or shying away. Once again, Irv had an eerie sense of recognition, of having seen that look before.

"Where you headed?" the girl asked, tossing her head back slightly as she spoke.

"I don't know," Irv answered. He leaned his elbows on his knees and looked back at her. "I woke up this morning and realized that I didn't want to live my life anymore. I decided I better find a new one, so here I am, trying to figure out where I want to go."

The girl considered Irv's reply for a moment and then shrugged her shoulder.

"That's fair," she said. "A lot of people don't really know where they're going, even though they think they do."

Irv felt a thin smile play across his face. "There is some truth to that," he said. "Where are you going?"

The girl twisted in her seat before she answered. "To San Diego to stay with my brother, Carlos. He has a cleaning business, and he said he would give me a job." She picked at the cover of the CD player, wiping at the logo with the raw end of a finger.

"Sounds like a good plan. Are you close to your brother?"

"No. I haven't seen him for six years."

Irv nodded his head.

"There are ten kids in my family," the girl continued. "My brother is the oldest, and I'm the youngest. I haven't been home in a while, so I called him and asked if I could come and stay with him. He said it was okay."

A deep male voice came over the loud speaker, announcing that the bus for Long Beach would board in ten minutes. On the television set mounted in the corner of the waiting area, Irv watched as Al Roker interviewed a lively group of Idaho teenagers who were visiting the city of New York for the first time. The girl took off the headphones that had been resting at the back of her neck and wrapped the cord around the CD player. When she leaned forward to put the player in the bag at her feet, Irv could see the hint of cleavage at the edge of her blouse, her skin brown and smooth above the neckline, making him aroused and sad at the same time.

The two of them silently watched the passengers alight from a northbound bus arriving from San Clemente.

"I had an older brother," Irv spoke, breaking the silence between them. "He died in the Korean War." He stopped and rubbed his fingers over the top part of his hands. "I was only fourteen when he died. He and my father fought all the time, about religion and such. My dad wanted him to be a rabbi, but Levi wanted to be a jazz musician. He was a wonderful piano player; could play Joplin, Morton, all the Ragtime greats. I never really got the chance to know him. Wish I was on my way to see him now."

The girl said nothing, looking out toward the station parking lot, her hands folded in her lap.

"The good thing about it is that my parents left me alone after Levi died. I guess his death provided them with enough guilt for the family. They never pressured me to do anything. Funny thing is, I thought about becoming a rabbi myself. Didn't like the studying, though. I was into sports: football, basketball, baseball. I spent most of my time outside, playing. I guess I wasn't happy unless I had a ball in my hands."

"So, what did you end up doing?" the girl asked.

"What? For work? Oh, a lot of different things. Went to college on a baseball scholarship, but I threw out my arm and had to give it up. I thought about being a sports writer, but I wasn't too good at the writing part. Ended up as a contract engineer. Ran a consulting firm for aerospace companies in the sixties. Retired a year ago."

"My dad works as a landscaper," the girl said. "He takes care of rich people's yards."

"What about your mother?' Irv asked.

"She's dead." The girl spoke softly, as if whispering a prayer.

"I'm sorry." Irv wanted to reach out and place his hand on her arm, but instead, he sat silently, watching his own hands as they trembled in his lap.

"What's your name?" he finally asked.

"Leticia Perez."

"I'm Irv Kaplan," he said.

Leticia smiled faintly as she shook his hand. Hers felt smooth and warm.

"What time does your bus leave for San Diego?"

"Three o'clock."

"That's a while from now. Do you want to go across the street and get a cup of coffee?" Irv hoped she would say yes and give him a reason to be present in this moment.

She hesitated, eyes cast down at the bag on the floor at her feet. Finally, she shrugged.

"Sure. Why not."

She and Irv crossed the street and entered Goodman's Deli. Inside, the restaurant was quiet, a few customers sitting at the stools at the deli counter. Irv and Leticia picked a booth in the back and then stared at the ten-page menus covered in laminated plastic. When the waitress appeared, Leticia ordered a hamburger, and a diet Coke; Irv asked for coffee and scrambled eggs. The two of them were quiet as the waitress brought their drinks. Irv stirred cream into his coffee and Leticia tentatively sipped her Coke, before breaking the silence.

"So, you have a wife and kids?"

"Yes and no,' Irv answered. "Wife; no kids. We wanted them but never had any luck. I think I'm the reason. Sperm count too low, or something like that."

Leticia smiled. "You were lucky," she said. "You wouldn't have wanted a family with as many kids as mine."

"Well, there are probably plusses and minuses. I always thought it would have been nice to have a son to play ball with. I'm sure Rose would have liked a daughter. Life doesn't always work out the way you want it to, though."

"You got that right," Leticia said, reaching for the ketchup bottle as the waitress set a hamburger in front of her. "I always thought that life would be different but, man, it's been good to no one. At least no one I know."

Irv pushed the scrambled eggs on his plate with his fork before looking up at Leticia. "That's a pretty pessimistic attitude for someone as young as you," he said.

"I'm not that young. I'm seventeen, going on eighteen. And I know more about life than a lot of people older than me." Leticia bit into her burger, wiping at the ketchup that leaked from the bottom of the bun. "Besides, look at you, you've lived your life and here you are telling me that you don't like it. What's up with that? You're the pessimistic one."

Irv thought a moment. What the girl said was true; he did feel his life had been a waste. Why was that? He wasn't certain; there could be so many reasons, really. But he didn't like this girl playing them back to him. He wanted to be in charge of his own despair.

"Well, I guess you have me there," Irv finally answered before taking a sip of his coffee. "The difference is that I've lived a long life—at least fifty years longer than yours—so it seems I'm entitled to a bit more regret than you. Your life is just beginning. Why do you have an edge on me there?"

"Shit, man, I don't have no edge on nobody." Leticia squeezed a blob of ketchup on her plate and stabbed at it with a French fry. "Where I come from, the boys are all in gangs. They skip school and drink, smoke dope. Some of them shoot horse. The girls are worse. They sleep with any boy they can so they can get pregnant and get away from their homes. My best friend, Anna, she got busted in a drug deal she was doing for her boyfriend. Now she's at a halfway house waiting to give her baby up for adoption. Our parents tell us 'stay in school,' 'don't do drugs,' but there's no point. We're all gonna end up like them anyway."

"But isn't that the reason to stay in school? So you can get an education? Make a better life for yourself than your father has?"

"Shit, there's no better life for someone like me. I can educate myself all I want, but the world's still gonna see me as a dumb chola. No one cares about me. Maybe if I was born in another time and another place, it'd be different. But, hey, I'm here. This is where I got thrown down."

The waitress brought the check and Irv reached into his gym bag for his wallet.

"But there are people who do bring themselves up from horrific circumstances. Look at all the Jews who were almost exterminated in World War II. They survived and went on to raise families and prosper again. Look at Abraham Lincoln, Albert Einstein, George Washington Carver. Hell, even Oprah Winfrey had a hard upbringing, endured physical abuse, and look she's built her own empire. Why can't you do that, too?"

Leticia looked off toward the window. When she turned back toward Irv, her eyes were old and tired.

"You don't understand, man. It's not that easy."

"Why not? I want to understand, believe me. Tell me why you have no hope."

Leticia picked up her bag and pulled it over her shoulder before standing up.

"Probably for the same reasons you don't," she said.

Leticia moved quietly to a corner of the hotel room and eased her jeans back on. She pulled her blouse over her head, and then tiptoed to the dresser to peer into Irv's gym bag. Inside she found his wallet, a baseball book, and a Dodgers jacket. Leticia looked back at the bed, where Irv breathed quietly, removed the wallet and opened it. Inside she found ten twenty-dollar bills, some credit cards, a 2001 Dodgers schedule, and a few photos. Leticia ran her finger over the sepia-colored shot of a white-haired couple, another photo of a much younger Irv and some woman—his wife, she guessed—in evening clothes. She took a few of the twenties and slipped them in her pocket, then closed the wallet and placed it back in the bag. She picked up her own bag and shoes and silently went out the door.

Once on the street, she took a deep breath and headed back toward the bus station. It was early morning and yesterday's three o'clock to San Diego was long gone. Maybe she could catch another one to San Clemente or Oceanside. If she hurried, maybe she could get close enough to San Diego to hitch a ride downtown. As she stepped into the station, she was met by an agitated crowd milling around the waiting area television set. On the screen, dark clouds

58

billowed from one of the World Trade Center towers in New York City. Leticia watched in disbelief as a small dark speck approached the second tower and ripped into the building, dragging behind it a burst of bright orange flames. The bus station crowd gave a collective gasp, many individuals cried out, and they all stood shocked and humbled at the drama unfolding before them on the small screen.

As the towers collapsed and CNN commentators rushed to decipher the meaning of what had just occurred on film before them, Leticia bowed her head, the words around her a dull roar. She thought of Irv, alone in the hotel room she had just left. He would wake up and see this horrific scene on TV. For some reason, the thought of him watching this alone filled her with shame and remorse. Gripping her bag tightly, she ran through the bus station entrance toward the hotel.

Irv woke with a start and sat up quickly in the creaky bed. The morning sun threw dusty streams of light through the hotel curtains, and he remembered where he was. He looked at the dresser, where his gym bag sat, and then at the floor, where his clothes lay in a pile, looking like a dismembered scarecrow. Where was Leticia? he wondered. Gone. Something might happen to her... she might be in danger without him. Then he remembered that she was from the streets; that nothing could scare her. He pushed back the bed sheet and stood up, his legs uncertain and weak.

Then Irv put his head in his hands and began to weep.

He wept for his parents, both dead and buried so far away that he could not place the stones on their gravesites. He wept for his brother, Levi, whom he had loved more than his father and whom he had never really known. He wept for Rose, for her constancy, her simplicity, her stubborn acceptance of the disappointments that life had offered her. He wept for the children he and Rose had never had, for his dreams of becoming a ball player, for the hundreds of minor disappointments that consumed him like rodents with small sharp teeth. He wept for Leticia, for her smooth young body, the magnificent roundness of her hips, her small delicate breasts, her soft mouth, her tender sighs as she slept. He wept for himself, for his weakness, for his self-consciousness, for his lack of joy.

Irv wept until he could weep no more and then, drawing a few deep breaths and running his hands over his gray hair, stumbled into the hotel bathroom and turned on the shower. He stepped inside and let the water wash over him. As the warm spray poured over his head and neck, he remembered taking showers at the gym when he was in high school. While washing the dirt and sweat of the game off his skin, he would replay every throw, every catch, every hit over and over, reliving the memories so that they would never leave him, never let him go.

When Irv got out of the shower, he picked his clothes up off the floor, shook them out and laid them carefully on the bed. He put on his favorite shirt, slipped on his khaki pants, tightened his belt and then tied his shoes. Using the hotel pen and stationary, he wrote a brief note to Leticia, 'You must find your strength in ancient sources,' he wrote. 'Stoicism, endurance, loyalty; they will stand you well. Otherwise, you can do nothing but confess your own bewilderment, and cower in silent wonder before the world.' He left it on the nightstand in case she came back, even though he guessed that by now, she would be far away, trying to escape the opportunities that life would never offer her.

Irv carried a chair out onto the hotel balcony and placed it next to the railing. He paused to gaze at the view of Los Angeles, in its gray, sprawling endlessness. For a brief moment, it seemed to Irv that the city held its breath, and then whispered its own sigh of loss and despair.

As the first knock sounded on his hotel room door, Irv stepped from the chair onto the railing of the balcony and leapt, stretching his arms out straight in front of him, in a perfect slide toward home.

HAVE YOU SEEN ME?

The first time I saw Allison, I didn't really see her at all.

I was walking up the stairs in the back entryway of my office building in San Diego. In my hurry to get to work that morning, my foot caught on one of the steps, and the stack of mail I was carrying suddenly slipped through my fingers and drifted down between the open gaps in the cement stairs. I remember clomping back down the stairway, my cowboy boots ringing loudly against each concrete platform. And I remember noticing, as I gathered the errant envelopes and flyers, a thin bedroll peeking out from under the vending machine that hummed in the corner. I didn't think much of it at the time; there was no security in the building, so wayward junk—

cigarette butts, empty food wrappers, even used syringes—was often left behind in our back entry by teenagers and homeless people who sometimes found their way there in the evening.

I gathered the fallen envelopes and headed back up the stairs to my office, where I work as a billing administrator for a group of doctors. I made a pot of strong coffee and, after firing up my computer, sat down at my desk to open the mail.

And that was the second time I saw Allison.

Sifting through the stack of correspondence, most of it addressed to me, Marilinda Greenwood, I came across one of those small flyers with pictures of missing children on them. Always interested in anything that has to do with the lost or lonely, I stopped and studied the black and white photograph, which showed a pale-faced young girl with kohl-rimmed eyes and bobbed hair. Below her name, Allison Jackman, the following details were listed in block print: DOB 1/3/1991, Height: 5'0', Weight: 100 lbs, Hair: Dk. Brown, Eyes: Brown, Sex: F, Date Missing: 5/5/2006, From: Tucson, AZ.

Whenever I receive one of these missing child flyers in the mail I linger over it, wondering about the child and the details of his or her disappearance. Was he abducted? Had she run away? Did any of them miss their mothers and their fathers, or were those the very people from whom they sought escape? At home, I tucked the mailers carefully into a drawer in the kitchen, periodically fishing them out and studying them to imprint the faces in my memory.

My dad laughed at me.

"If you wanted to have kids, you should have done it the old-fashioned way," he said one afternoon, when I showed him a particularly sad photo of a twelve-year-old boy from Pittsburgh, who had been missing for three years.

What he meant was that I should have gotten married and started a family when I had the chance twenty years ago, instead of being a forty-year-old singleton living with her widowed father in a three bedroom house in Rancho Bernardo.

But I've never been a believer in luck or chance; I've always thought that I could make things happen myself if I tried hard enough. And if they didn't happen, then maybe they weren't right for me in the first place.

At least, that's what I've told myself all these years.

I didn't think about Allison again until late in the day, when the afternoon sun came slanting through the blinds in my office, lacing the spreadsheet on my desk with thin bands of white light. I'd spent most of the day computing payroll taxes, taking an almost sinful pleasure in writing numbers on tax coupons, so I didn't notice the time as it flew by that afternoon. I loved computing percentages and totaling work hours, my fingers dancing over the keyboard on my adding machine, the delicious satisfaction of numbers adding up. I tore off strips of white adding machine tape, ran Xerox copies, licked envelopes, and carefully filed each monthly report. Although I had done this job for thirteen years, I never tired of these tasks, so simple and measurable and anchored in their execution.

So when I finally glanced at the clock that afternoon, it was already three-thirty. But if I hurried, I would still have time to grab a coffee at Starbucks before heading out to Escondido, where I volunteer at the local animal shelter. I gathered my purse and keys, taking a moment to stuff the missing children announcement into my pocket. After shutting down my computer, I turned out the light and hurried down the back steps of the building.

As I swung open the door to the parking lot, I spotted a girl smoking a cigarette near the dumpster by the back fence. I didn't get a good look at her face, but I did see dark, short hair and the protective way she hugged one arm to her waist as she lifted the cigarette to her lips with the other. She wore a navy blue sweater and a pair of baggy sweatpants. Gazing up at the sky, as if purposely avoiding any eye contact with me, she exhaled a perfect ring of wavy gray smoke as I rushed by her to my car.

It was only while I was backing out of my parking spot near the door that I realized this might be the girl on the flyer. I glanced up at my rear view mirror, but she was no longer in sight. A car came up close behind me, preventing me from stopping or turning around, so I exited the parking lot. As I waited for the signal to change on Clairemont Mesa Boulevard, I thought about the odds. Arizona wasn't that far from California, and the person in the photo had disappeared about nine months before, which was certainly enough time to make her way to San Diego.

At Starbucks, my favorite barista, Hector, greeted me from behind the register.

"Marrrileeenda!" he crowed, pronouncing my name with the same rolling r's that my Spanish-French mother had used. "Look, Reggie, it's the

Rabbit Whisperer, rescuer of all the lost bunnies in San Diego!"

His boyfriend, Reggie, a thin man with a shaved head and a tiny gold ring in his right earlobe, allowed himself the briefest nod in my direction.

"Will it be your usual today?" Hector flashed a row of white teeth. "Grande, sugar-free cinnamon dulce, no whip?" Before I had time to say yes, he leaned over the counter and stage whispered, "I'll make it for you myself."

While he prepared my drink, Hector babbled cheerfully. He was a theater major at San Diego State University, and worked at this particular Starbuck's because, like me, he still lived at home in nearby University City. His parents didn't know about Reggie, I was sure.

"Hey, Hector," I said, as he handed me my coffee. "Do you ever see any of the kids on these flyers?" I held up the notice with Allison's picture on it.

Hector took the paper from my hand.

"No," he said. "How about you, Reggie?"

Reggie ambled over and peered past Hector's shoulder at the mailer.

"Sometimes kids come in who are obvious runaways," he said. "A few of them work the strip

68

club down the street. But I've never seen this one." He looked up at me, his eyes a cool green. "Why, have you seen this girl?"

"I don't know," I said, taking the flyer back from Hector and slipping it into my pocket. "I may have."

"Well," Hector said, "if you do, bring her in; I'll make her a nice hot chocolate!"

I thought about his remark as I battled the already heavy traffic on the freeway to the shelter. What would I say if it was her? And how likely would it be that I'd "bring her in" anywhere? As I navigated through the endless lights on Valley Center, I wondered if people ever recognized kids on these flyers. It was something I'd have to look into when I got home.

The animal shelter sits at the far end of Escondido, nestled up against the base of the San Marcos foothills in a small clearing surrounded by new housing developments. Even though it's located in the middle of an older North County suburb, the shelter's plot of land has the look of a western ranch, with a few scraggly manzanita bushes dotting an adjacent field of scattered rocks and dirt. After parking in the nearly empty lot, I took a moment to breathe in the quiet majesty of the rocky hillside and the warmth of the February sunlight before gathering my bag of supplies, which included white vinegar, rubbing alcohol, scotch tape, and miscellaneous chew toys.

When I opened the shelter door, I was hit with the acrid smell of cat urine and the echoing bark of the dogs in the back kennel. Arlene and Cassie, the two front desk volunteers, barely glanced at me. The two older ladies stood huddled together near the gift shop entrance, most likely discussing some bit of celebrity gossip in the magazine Arlene held in her hands.

After a mumbled hello, which they barely acknowledged, I pulled my ID card and door key out of the volunteer supervisor's desk and walked through the corridor of the cat housing to the tiny back room which served as the rabbit area. When I came in, the rabbits stared at me forlornly through the bars of their cages. They occupied twenty seven of the forty pens, which were stacked in columns of four against each of the walls of the room. Some of the bunnies hopped over to their doors as I called out their names, pushing their noses through the bars in hopes that I'd let them out or offer them treats.

After donning an apron and spending a few moments greeting each of them, I lifted a large white

Dutch named Bailey out of his cage, and set him inside the small corral that functioned as an exercise area. I gave Bailey a toilet paper roll stuffed with hay and a brown paper bag to play with and then turned to the two large barrels, one full of timothy hay and one for trash, in the center of the room. There was no light fixture in the rabbit area, only a bank of windows that let in a small amount of illumination. I had to work fast before the sun went down and plunged the room into darkness.

As I emptied trays and filled the rabbits' cages with fresh hay, one of the employees, a shy teenager with Down's syndrome named Ellen, burst through the door, waving a newspaper in her hand.

"Look, Mari, you're in the *North County Times*!" she whispered excitedly.

I wiped my hands on my apron and took the paper from her. There I was, indeed, clutching a large white rabbit named Theo to my breast. I remembered when this photograph was taken; it was during a celebration for the opening of the new shelter after the old one was destroyed in a wildfire that had swept through the county three years ago.

I studied my face in the photo, hating my large nose, smiling at the startled look in my eyes. But what struck me most of all was how much I was beginning to look like my mother when she was my age. I had the same unruly dark hair, chopped bluntly and resting loosely on my shoulders, the same pointed chin, the same lines around my mouth when frowning, which I appeared to be doing in the photo. I also noticed the copious amount of gray that appeared at my temples. It was time to use some hair color.

"Thanks, Ellen." I handed her the newspaper and went back to cleaning trays.

"Did you see the new bunny in the holding area?" she asked.

"No, I haven't had a chance to go out there, but I'll take a look in a moment."

I wasn't happy to hear that there was a new rabbit at the shelter. With funding and staff time limited, the bunnies ended up the lowest animals in the rescue hierarchy, receiving little attention from the hired staff and no chance of neutering from the veterinarians who donated their time there. I knew that this new rabbit would sit for months, just like the others, waiting for someone to adopt it. Most likely it was white, which for some reason seemed to be the favorite color for those abandoning a rabbit, and the least popular amongst potential adopters.

I finished the trays in the fading sunlight, and swapped out Bailey for a bonded pair of lops named

Ruby and Dusty, and then took a quick jog back to the holding area, a small sagging wooden building with twelve empty cages, where recently abandoned animals were held for treatment and observation before being moved inside the shelter. There in the back corner, just as I suspected, sat a medium-sized white rabbit with a bit of gray on its ears and back, cowering against the far side of its cage. It wiggled its nose at me as I pushed my finger through the bars to stroke the back of its fur. It seemed gentle and looked healthy, though a bit thin. So sad that someone could dump a creature that was so perfect and sweet.

I was about to leave the holding area when the bunny turned in its cage, and I saw a streak of something red and wet-looking on the fur near its tail. Coming closer, I noticed a brown mass in the corner of the cage. Another one appeared a moment later, and I realized that this rabbit was giving birth.

"Arlene, Ellen!" I called toward the main building but, when no one answered, I ran back to the health center inside and pushed open the door. At five thirty in the evening, none of the staff or volunteer vets was there. I raced up to the front of the office and found Arlene and Cassie filling small baggies with dog biscuits for the gift shop.

"The new rabbit's giving birth in the holding pen," I said.

Arlene set down the bag she was tying off with a bit of raffia and looked at me.

"Well, Ellen's the only one here right now. Why don't the two of you find a box for the babies, and we'll leave a note for the med team in the morning."

"Right." Not wanting to take the time to find Ellen, I decided to handle this incident myself and raced back to the holding pen. Nothing had changed since I'd left. The two newborns, which looked like small brown baby birds, barely moved on the bottom of the cage, while the mother sat quietly hunched in the corner.

I hurried to the stock room in the back of the shelter and found an empty box that would fit inside the cage. After lining it with a clean rag from the laundry room, I ran back to the holding area. Like the rabbit room inside the shelter, the holding pen had no electric lighting. The sun had begun to set and the room was growing dark.

I peered through the bars and could still make out the rabbit, who had backed up against the corner of her cage. She didn't seem to mind when I placed the box inside. I reached in and carefully scooped up the two babies, who felt sticky and cold against the palm of my hand, and set them gently inside the box. The mother ignored them, gazing at me with glassy blue eyes that almost seemed to glitter in the growing darkness. I knew that rabbits usually gave birth to six to eight kits and that these two were the first wave of the litter. It would probably take the mother all night to birth the remaining babies.

After making sure that she had a fresh bottle of water and plenty of kibble and hay, I went back into the main building to finish up with the rest of the rabbits. Before I left, I documented my chores on a clipboard for the next day's volunteers and wrote a note to the shelter's health center staff to alert them to the newborns in the holding pen.

When I finally left the shelter, it was dark outside. A rounded sliver of new moon, looking silvery and wan, peeked tiredly over the top of the hills. Although it had been a long and exhausting afternoon, I felt strangely elated by the day's events. As I started the car, I realized that in all the excitement with the new rabbit, I hadn't thought at all about the teenager I'd seen in the parking lot after work. I wondered where she slept in the evening and if the bedroll I'd seen stashed under the vending machine was hers.

I was tempted to drive over to the building to check and see if she was there, but my stomach growled suddenly, reminding me that I hadn't eaten since noon. Dad would be waiting for me to fix him dinner. A wave of fatigue washed over me and I decided, reluctantly, that I would have to look for Allison tomorrow.

With the feel of the newborn kits still lingering in the palm of my hand, I pulled out of the lot and steered my car down the dark road toward home.

The houses in our neighborhood huddled together at the east end of Rancho Bernardo, a worn group of one-story houses with faded red-tile roofs and yellowing stucco meant to be Spanish styled, now looking sadly dated. Many of the tiny lawns were dotted with white rocks instead of grass to ease the landscaping burden of the seniors who lived there. Ours was easy to pick out in the evening darkness; the collection of Malibu lights glimmered like a constellation of tiny blue stars leading to our front door. I pulled into the driveway and the garage door swung open to reveal my father, in a rusty plaid shirt and stained overalls, standing at his workbench, roughing out a block of limestone with a heavy chisel. He wore safety goggles, a monkey mask, and leather gloves, a ghostly surgeon in the greenish glow of the overhead fluorescent lights. He didn't turn around when I parked the car next to him, continuing to bang the mallet against the chisel, knocking large chunks of stone onto the cement floor.

I picked up a pair of safety glasses from the workbench and leaned in next to him. "What will this one be?' I asked.

"I don't know," he said. "I'm thinking a Buddha, but I can't be sure until I get more of it carved off here."

I watched him work for a few minutes, noticing how steady his hands were, despite his seventy years. His face had the same thoughtful expression he always wore when he was serious about something. It was a look of kindness and long-suffering patience, forged from years of taking care of other people—his students at the high school where he once taught social studies classes, my mother, in the last few years of her battle with breast cancer. During his retirement he'd taken up sculpture, graduating from small bits of soapstone to larger blocks of alabaster and Italian Carrera marble. His work adorned our living room and the back yard garden, peopling our property with a one-man show of busts, torsos, and statues of various animals, their limbs frozen in mid-motion, as if cast in stone by some mischievous magician.

"There was a new rabbit at the shelter tonight," I said. "I got to watch it give birth to two babies."

My father grunted. He was allergic to cats, a convenient excuse for not allowing me to have pets at the house.

"You spend so much time there," he said. "I'm surprised you don't give birth to a few rabbits yourself."

"It's not that much time," I said. "And if I wanted to give birth, it would be to something better than a rabbit."

"I thought nothing was better than a rabbit," he replied, the hint of a smile in his voice. He tapped away the last corner of the gray block so that a curved edge suddenly emerged, giving the piece the look of a bare human's rounded back rising from a bed of stone.

"I'm starting to see your Buddha," I said.

"He's in there," he answered, laying down the heavy chisel and picking through the tools scattered on his workbench. He pushed aside his coping saw and rifflers until he unearthed a point chisel, one that was covered, like everything else in the garage, with a fine layer of dust. Holding it at a forty-five degree angle, he began to tap out a line in the stone.

"How will you know when it's done?" I asked.

"When I fall in love with it," he answered. Without looking up or pausing, he rhythmically coaxed a curved limb from the piece of stone.

I left him to his dust and his half-born Buddha and went into the house to fix something to eat. While I chopped some cooked chicken and arranged bright green spears of romaine in a salad bowl, the doorbell rang, announcing the arrival of my boyfriend, Milo. When I opened the door, he gave me his usual disheveled smile, then pulled me close, lifting me slightly off the floor in a one-armed hug, his dark beard like a stiff brush tickling my neck, his shirt giving off the slightly musty smell of weed. In one hand he held a medium-sized pet carrier.

"You're early," I said. I took the carrier from him and closed the door.

"Happy Valentine's Day," he replied, handing me a small box wrapped in gold paper with a red ribbon around it.

"But it's not Valentine's Day yet." I shook the box slightly to see if I could figure out what was inside.

"That's all right," he said. "I have to work tomorrow night, so we can celebrate today."

"Should I open this now, or save it for later?" I spoke these words over my shoulder, as Milo followed me into the kitchen.

"Later," he answered, lingering over the word in a way that told me ours would be a private celebration.

I set the carrier on the floor and pulled the latch open. Benjy, a coffee-colored lop-eared Dutch, emerged cautiously, his large black nose quivering as he headed directly for the dining room table. He immediately hunkered down and began to nibble the carpet, stopping once to give a loud thump with his hind leg. Milo and I shared him in what can best be described as a kind of joint custody arrangement since Benjy's discovery two years ago by friends of mine. He'd been dumped in the parking lot at the canyon preserve near Scripps Ranch, with a pile of lettuce and a carrot next to him. Being a fairly well-fed domestic rabbit, he'd been too slow to elude my friend's son, who caught him and brought him home in a cardboard box, where they kept him until I convinced them to let me take him home. After two weeks at our house, when my father could no longer tolerate the mess or the smell of hay, Milo offered to keep Benjy at his apartment downtown, bringing him over for visits once a week, or whenever Milo felt the need to spend time with me.

I set three plates at the table and served the Caesar chicken salad with a chilled bottle of sauvignon blanc from the Rancho Bernardo Winery.

Dad joined us at the table, giving Milo a brief nod of acknowledgement and deliberately ignoring Benjy, who sat on a piece of carpet in the kitchen, nibbling at a chunk of carrot. We humans dined quietly, sipping our drinks and not saying much until most of the food was gone.

After pushing his empty plate away, my father drained the last of his wine, then paused and looked over at Milo.

"Anything hot come over the wire this week?" he asked.

"No," Milo answered, wiping his mouth with his napkin and throwing me a quick grin. He knew that my dad, despite not caring for him much, was hooked on the stories he told about the calls he received as a 911 dispatcher. "Although I did get one today from a woman who had a spider in her bathtub."

"What?" I stood to clear the plates. "You're kidding, right?"

"No," he answered. "This woman was screaming that there was a spider on the wall. She wanted me to come over and kill it for her."

"Bet you would have enjoyed that," I said.

Milo laughed. "Yeah, she was pretty riled up. She had this heavy accent and she kept yelling 'There it is! There it is!'

"What did you tell her?" my dad asked.

"I asked her if she needed any assistance, but she kept screaming 'It's climbing down my wall; there it is, over there!'" He chuckled. "Then she yelled 'Get it! Get it!'" and slammed down the receiver before I could say anything." He shook his head and took a sip of wine.

"That's pretty good," my father said.

"Yeah," Milo said. He paused a moment. "The rest of the night was more typical. A lot of drunks coming after their wives." He drained his glass and handed it to me as I gathered the last of the silverware from the table.

"What about your day, Mari?" Milo asked. "Anything interesting happening with the doctors?"

"Well, yes," I said. I brought in a plate of shortbread, setting it in front of Milo and out of my dad's reach. My father immediately leaned over and grabbed two of the cookies. "I saw this girl today." I handed Milo the flier from my pocket.

My dad rolled his eyes. "Not the lost kids again."

"But I really saw one today, Dad. In the flesh. The real thing." I picked up a cookie and nibbled on it, then set in on the napkin in front of me.

"Are you sure it was this girl?" Milo asked.

82

I took the flier back from him. Allison's face stared up at me, a distant, haunted look in her eyes. I suddenly recalled the scent, acrid and sooty, of the perfect ring of smoke she'd exhaled as I walked by.

"Yes," I said. "I think so."

"Well," my father said, "we're sure to meet her, then. You'll be bringing her home and asking me if she can stay here." He reached for another cookie and then waved it at me as he spoke. "You're just like your mother, you know. She was always trying to save any wretched thing she met on the street."

Milo raised his glass. "To Mari," he said, "the rescuer."

The three of us clinked our glasses together. As I sipped my wine, I kept my eyes on my father, who studiously avoided my gaze.

He and I both knew that my mother hadn't been like that at all.

Later, I lay on my bed, my arm stretched back against the pillows, and watched Milo smoke a joint in the chair near my bedroom window. His eyes were half-lidded and dreamy, as if his thoughts were far away. I noticed how long his hair had gotten, the dark curls sprawling across the collar of his shirt. He sucked at the bud in his fingers, the ashes flaring bright orange against the paper, and then held his breath for a moment before finally releasing a stream of pale smoke through his nostrils and mouth. The strong weedy scent lingered in the air. Healthy and strong, he was so different from the thin, sniffling man who'd appeared at our door two years ago with a bag of grass in his pocket for my mother.

"Why does your father do that?" he asked.

"Do what?"

"Idealize your mother," he said. It was as if he had read my mind, the memory of her suddenly hovering, a ghostly presence in my bedroom.

I thought for a moment. "I guess that's what people do when they love each other," I said.

"Do you idealize me?" He reached across to the tiny desk and tamped out the joint stub on a large seashell next to my laptop. After closing the window, he came over to the bed and placed his hand on the top of my leg. The heat of his palm felt warm through my jeans.

"Why would I do that?" I answered, reaching up to kiss him, his lips soft and sooty-tasting, his arms feeling thick and firm through his shirt. My mother's ghostly presence vanished in a puff of smoke.

Milo and I made love, quick and sure. Afterward, we lay quietly side by side, my arm across his chest.

"Happy Valentine's Day," he said. "You should open your present."

We'd brought Benjy, now snug in his carrier, and the gift upstairs with us after dinner. The present sat on top of Benjy's cage in the corner. I threw off the sheets and tiptoed over to it, gathering the gift and then stopping at my dresser to open a drawer and remove something I'd bought Milo. It wasn't much— a tin of chocolate-covered pretzels, wrapped in white tissue paper and a red ribbon.

"Here," I said, "open yours first."

He peeled off the tissue and then smiled when he saw the label.

"It's because you like salty things so much," I said, wishing the gift had been more glamorous.

He opened the lid and the sweet scent of chocolate filled the room. He leaned back against the pillow, munching on a twist.

"Your turn," he said.

I took the tiny box, slipped the ribbon off, and ran my finger under the shiny gold foil. Inside, on a small pad of cotton, lay a bracelet made up of multi-colored stones interspersed with tiny wooden beads.

Attached was a small tag with the words "unexpected miracles" printed across it, fortune cookie style, in faded blue lettering.

I didn't speak as I lifted the bracelet and studied the beads in the lamp light.

"They're karma beads," Milo said. "They'll bring you good luck."

"Thank you," I whispered. I slipped the bracelet on my wrist and then leaned back down and kissed him.

"You should move in with me," he said.

I didn't answer. We'd had this conversation many times before.

After a few moments, he spoke again.

"Really, Mari, it's time. Al is doing fine now; he needs to have his own life and you need yours."

Once more, I said nothing. My own life consisted of a limited job, a lonely father, and a boyfriend who worked as a telephone operator. I wasn't sure if any of it was what I needed. But my needs were my own business.

"Your place is too small," I finally answered. "You don't have room for me there." This much was true; we joked about Milo's studio apartment, which I referred to as "the hole" because of its subterranean downstairs location and lack of light.

I ran my finger across the middle of his chest, then rested my hand near his heart. I could feel the faint thump of its beat, soft and steady against my palm.

"And Dad needs me. It may not seem like it to you, but it's important that I'm here for him."

"What if I need you, too?"

I turned my head on the pillow and looked over at him. His eyes were closed, the dark lashes resting on his cheek, his mouth like the petals of a flower, a soft raspberry pink against his beard.

"Don't guilt me like that, Milo." I said. "I do enough of that to myself."

He was quiet a moment, and then sat up, the movement pulling the sheet away from my stomach. The room suddenly felt cold.

"Fine," he said.

He stood and wrestled into his jeans and shirt, then picked up Benjy's carrier and reached for the door. He turned and gazed at me a moment, with a pure, open expression on his face. Then the door closed behind him.

I laid on the bed, studying the maroon, green, and lavender beads of my bracelet. I knew that Milo would sulk for a few days and then return, grudgingly accepting my terms, for the time being. I wondered how long his love for me would hold out.

If there were unexpected miracles in my life, Milo was certainly one of them. Perhaps Allison would be another.

I reached for the bedside lamp and turned off the light with a sharp click.

I am not a morning person. Never have been, according to my father, who said that my mother once poured a glass of water on my head to get me up for school one day when I was little. I don't recall that incident; for some reason, many of my childhood memories appear blurry and unreachable to me now, as if they didn't even happen.

But as I splashed water on my face the morning after Milo's visit, I felt strangely awake; I might see Allison. I hurried through my shower and breakfast, quickly choking down a piece of dry toast and largely ignoring my father's attempts at conversation in the kitchen, where I tossed an apple and a bagel into a brown lunch bag. I gave Dad a quick kiss on the top of his head while he read the paper, and then hurried out to my car, doing my best to keep my foot off the accelerator once I was on the freeway. After watching for the highway patrolman who liked to hide his motorcycle below the overpass for Highway 52, I found the Clairemont Mesa exit and headed to my building.

When I pulled into the potted driveway, I felt a sharp little pinprick of excitement as I scanned the parking lot for signs of Allison. But, aside from a few scattered cigarette butts next to the dumpster, there was no sign of her anywhere, even in the stairwell, where the vending machine hummed wearily as I clomped my way upstairs, my cowboy boots creating a hollow echo against the cement steps.

Later in the afternoon, I carried the payroll tax stubs downstairs to my clients' office, which sits on the lower floor of the building, along the south face toward the back lot. The tiny waiting room was quiet, only an older woman and her teenaged son, his foot in a soft cast, sat in the wicker chairs lined against the wall. Myra, the receptionist, kept me at the counter, her comments about a reality show she had seen last night on television punctuated with a raspy smokers' cough.

"That one black singer, she's good," Myra announced. She didn't look up from her keyboard as she spoke, her shoulders hunched against her polyester shirt collar, a pair of spectacles perched on her long brown nose, the beaded strap connected to the ends of her glasses swaying against her cheeks. "She's a big girl, so she can belt it. Not like those skinny white chicks; they sound like chickens squawking."

I smiled at her as I set the payroll tax envelope on the counter, next to a half-empty bowl of candy hearts, the pale chalky looking ones with sayings on them like "Be Mine," or "Too Cute."

"Remind Dr. Harris that these need to be paid tomorrow," I said.

"Okay." Myra coughed into her hand. "I have some workman's comp forms he said to give you."

As she rummaged through the stack of papers her desk, I glanced out the tiny window behind her and then froze. There was the girl I had seen yesterday, her hand cupped around a cigarette as she tried to light it.

"Quick, Myra, give me one of your Pall Malls."

"When did you start smoking?." She looked at me dubiously, her upturned eyes narrowing into a squint.

"Just give me one," I answered, thrusting my hand out toward her.

She opened a desk drawer and reluctantly fished one out of her purse. I grabbed the smoke. "Thanks.

I'll be back in a minute for those forms," I added hastily, than rushed out to the back door and shoved it open.

The girl turned around and gave me the briefest once over as I stepped out into the parking lot, then took a few steps away toward the dumpster and stood there with her back to me. The sky glowered above us, a sullen blanket of overcast cloudiness.

"Hey," I said, trying to sound nonchalant. "Could I bum a light from you?"

She turned back toward me and paused a moment, as if trying to decide whether I was worth acknowledgement. I noticed that she wore the same navy sweater and sweats as yesterday, her feet encased in a frayed pair of black Keds.

"Yeah, sure," she said. She fished in her pocket and handed me a lighter, its red plastic sides slimy and smooth. I noticed that her fingernails, covered with chipped black polish, were bitten to the quick.

"Thanks," I stuck the cigarette in my mouth, and then bit down to hold it steady, trying not to appear awkward as I flipped the lighter switch a couple of times before getting the end to light.

I handed the lighter back to her and then tried not cough as I took a drag on the filter tip. The smoke burned the back of my throat and felt as if it had surged right down into my lungs. I choked back the first cough and then gave in, hacking like a grade-schooler sneaking her first cigarette.

"You all right?" she asked, pushing an expert stream of white smoke out of the side of her mouth.

"Yeah," I wheezed, as I banged the front of my chest with my fist. After pounding my sternum a few times, I cleared my throat and flicked at the end of the cigarette in my hand, trying to loosen enough of it so that it would burn down more quickly. "Just went down the wrong pipe."

She said nothing, taking another hit of her smoke and then gazing up at the sky, as if there were an important message written up there in the clouds for her to read.

"I haven't seen you before," I spoke casually, attempting a conversational tone. "You work here?"

She paused again before answering, as if considering whether she should share any information with a total stranger.

"No," she said.

I waited for more, but nothing came from her. Convinced even more that she was the girl I'd seen on the flyer, I decided to try to keep her talking.

"I do," I said. I pointed toward the second floor windows. "I work up there, in 206."

She followed my outstretched hand with her gaze, and took another hit of her cigarette. After a quick exhale, she tossed the butt to the concrete and ground it under her heel.

"Gotta run," she said, then turned and started walking toward the street end of the lot.

"Wait!" I cried out before even considering what I was going to say next.

She turned back toward me, her arms wrapped around her waist in the same protective manner I'd noticed yesterday.

I stood there, wondering what I could say that would keep her there.

"Have you had lunch yet?" I asked. Before she could answer, I continued, babbling so quickly my words tumbled over themselves. "Because I haven't eaten and I've got a bunch of stuff upstairs. We could have sandwiches or soup, I have soup, would you like some?" I stopped, feeling like an utter idiot and hoping she would be hungry enough to take me up on it.

She said nothing at first, and then glanced up at the second story windows, as if considering the distance she would have to climb to go up there.

"I've got plenty," I said. "It will only take a moment to fix." I hoped she didn't notice the pleading tone that had crept into my voice.

As I spoke, I studied her face. She had a thin spray of freckles on her nose, and three sets of tiny silver studs in a trail up each ear. The eyeliner under her lashes was smudged below each eye, giving her a tired, waifish appearance. I knew that she was definitely the girl in the photograph.

She gave her shoulders a tired shrug. "Okay," she said.

And then a miraculous thing happened—she smiled. It was the barest hint of a smile, but I saw it there, tugging at the corners of her mouth.

I led her through the back door and up the stairway, hiding, as best I could, my own emerging grin.

LABRADOR BLUES

It was my younger brother, Josh, who bet me that I wouldn't meet the woman of my dreams before my twenty-fifth birthday.

"You're relationship-challenged, Les," he pronounced one night over a couple of beers at Seau's, after I'd let two gorgeous cheerleader types get away without acquiring a phone number.

He was right; I'd never had good luck with girls. I don't know why that is, really. My female friends tell me I'm good-looking enough (all right, it was my mom and my sister who said it, but they *are* female). And I have dated women. I even had a girlfriend, Brenda, who I saw exclusively for two years. But something always seems to get in the way. With

Brenda it was religion. I couldn't get into the Sunday church thing or her father's preaching at the dinner table. With my other girlfriends, after a few boring dates and fumbling nights in my car or their dorm rooms, I was ready to move on. Now that I was out of school and had a job, it seemed easier to spend my time running or riding my bike. Cheaper, too.

But I secretly wished I had a real girlfriend. I'd watch Josh holding hands and joking around with Lana, a really sweet grad student at State, and I'd tell myself I could love someone like that. So, when Josh came up with the bet, I was ready to take him on. I told him I had a secret weapon and bet him a case of Michelob that I would meet the woman who was destined to be my wife by November 22nd, my birthday. Never mind that I didn't have a secret weapon when I made the bet. I had something better: my co-worker, Jamie, who was cool and brilliant and a lesbian. Jamie would figure out what I needed to do because she knew women better than I knew the back of my Corvette convertible.

I decided to approach Jamie when I was one month away from having to pay up. We had worked together for two years at MicroDataStream, a software company in Mission Valley, and we knew each other pretty well. She was familiar with my losing streak with women, and I had nursed her through a rough breakup with her last girlfriend, Kristina. Jamie was pretty destroyed over it, but she got out there and hustled up a new girlfriend, Monica, within a month. I figured she knew what she was doing, at least enough to advise the likes of me.

"Jamie, I need your help." I sidled up to her computer and placed a steaming mocha latte from Starbucks next to her keyboard.

"Don't try to bribe me, Lester, I'm on deadline." Jamie continued to stare at her computer screen, even though she picked up the coffee and took a sip. "Besides, you owe me for the football pool and lunch last week, so shouldn't I be the one demanding favors?"

"This is big. Really big." I leaned in close and whispered slowly in her ear. "It involves my personal life."

Jamie sat up straight and tore her eyes away from the screen.

"You finally got a life?" she responded. "I *do* have to hear this."

Pleased that my ploy had worked, I described the bet and the approaching deadline.

"Look you're a single, twenty-something female," I said as Jamie rolled her eyes toward the ceiling. "No, really, you're a woman, you know what women want. Just tell me what I need to do to find one, uh, really fast."

"You never learn do you," she answered, turning back to her computer. 'Women want the same thing men want. We want to be loved, and appreciated, and treated like human beings. Someday, when you figure that out, you'll find one. Maybe one with a brain, even. And God help her if she thinks she's going to enjoy spending her life with you."

I spun her chair around so that she had to face me. "C'mon," I said, "I need help here. What would you do if you had a month to meet a girl?"

Jamie picked up the coffee cup and put it to her lips. I watched as she reached up and ran a hand over her curly blond hair.

"Well that's easy, Les." She paused a moment, then looked up at me with a blazing smile. "I'd get a dog."

A dog? I had to think about that one. I mean I'm OK with animals. I recall even owning a gerbil once when I was a kid. But a dog? That was a big commitment. You had to walk them and feed them and take them to the vet when they were sick. I wouldn't even bring my car into the shop unless it had stopped cold, so what would I do with a dog that could get sick on me, a dog that would force me to care about something other than myself?

"Oh, thanks, that's a big help. Why would I need a dog to meet women?" I stood by her desk and scratched my head. "Do girls really *like* dogs?"

Jamie smiled as she tapped her keyboard. She was enjoying this a little too much.

"Trust me. If you want to meet a girl in a month, get a dog. Take it down to Dog Beach and walk it after work. I promise, you'll meet somebody decent." Jamie stood up, grabbed the coffee and her cell phone and headed off to the conference room for a standing 10:00 meeting with the boss.

A dog, I thought to myself. My secret weapon, a canine. I shook my head. Well, if that's what it took to land the woman of my dreams, bring it on. A dog owner I would be.

"We don't allow no dogs here, Meester Vitek." Rosa Morales, the landlady at my apartment in Mission Hills was having one of her famous hot flashes. With one hand, she fanned her flushed face and neck vigorously with a *People* magazine, while the other jangled a set of keys that would make Quasimodo swoon. We were standing in the laundry room as she energetically ripped into the locks on the washing machines.

"But it's only for a little while," I yelled over the din while quarters poured from each machine into a Folgers coffee can.

"The neighbors see you with a dog, and pretty soon, everybody want one."

"But, I have a ground floor apartment. I'll keep it inside, I swear, no one will know about it." I lowered my lip and drooped my eyes in my best puppy dog imitation. Rosa loved me, I knew she did. She slapped together fresh, hot tortillas every week in her apartment and handed me a steaming bag of them on my way home from work on Fridays. Every Christmas she brought me a basket of her handmade tamales, wrapped in a warm towel. She told me what a good boy I was and how she wished she had a son like me. She, of all people, would let me have my way.

I looked at her pleadingly, with all the manipulation I could muster. Rosa finally stopped rattling the coffee can and glared at me in exasperation.

"Okay, I let this go this one time. But you got to promise me if anyone complains, the dog is gone, right away."

"Thank you, Rosa, thank you." I hugged her tightly, which made her flush even more. "There will be no problems. Promise."

I whistled as I walked back to my apartment. One major hurdle down. Now all I had to do was figure out where I would put a dog.

"Toxic waste dump," Jamie called it.

"A disgrace," my mother christened it, after her one and only visit.

Okay, so it needed a little cleaning. A Trek mountain bike, my prize possession, had the premier spot in the center of the living room. It was upside down on a spread-out newspaper, with tools and old inner tubes scattered on the floor. This week's laundry was piled on the hand-me-down sofa, and last night's dinner remains -- a Healthy Choice frozen meal tray, a Corona bottle, and an empty Hagen-Das carton -- lay strewn on the coffee table. A dog wouldn't mind all this, I told myself. Yeah, but a girl with half a brain would, I could hear Jamie saying in my inner ear. Enough self-doubt, I told myself. If chez Lester was good enough for me, it would be good enough for my canine babe magnet and the women who would stream through my door. Sure, if all you want is *good enough*, Jamie's taunting voice echoed in my imagination.

So, that was how I ended up leaving the Labrador Rescue Center with Sally. She was a full-grown black lab with a sad look and a load of buckshot in her hindquarters.

"Some inhuman beast really abused this animal," the woman behind the counter said to me as I wrote out a check. "She's lucky to have a kind person like you to care for her." The woman gave me a glowing look with big, watery eyes that said "God bless you" behind her tortoiseshell glasses. I was tempted to tell her the truth: the only reason I was taking the dog was because I was about to lose a bet, but better judgment prevailed and I resisted the urge to share. On my way home, I stopped at PetCo and bought a thick red leash, a muzzle with the irresistible brand name *Behave*, and a bag of Iams dog food. I was now a full-fledged dog owner, though I didn't know a thing about owning a dog.

When we got home, Sally stopped in front of the mountain bike and sat on her haunches.

"Come on, girl. Come here." I slapped my hand gently against the leg of my jeans and beckoned to her. "Come on."

Sally looked at me without moving, jaws drooping, tongue hanging out.

So, this was supposed to stop women dead in their tracks? The enormity of the joke Jamie had played on me struck me with full force. Well, I'd show her. And Josh, too. I'd go out there and meet a woman if it was the last thing I did in my twenty-fourth year.

The first attempt was Sabrina, and she owned a humungous gray standard poodle named Bitsy.

"Oh, look, they're sniffing each other," Sabrina pointed out, as if I hadn't noticed. She was gorgeous. Thick black hair down to her butt and a smooth brown navel that would have turned J.Lo green with envy. Our dogs circled each other nose to rear, as only dogs can do, while Sabrina and I sized each other up.

"Hi, I'm Les Vitek." Not the brightest opening line, but I didn't know how else to respond to the sniffing comment.

"Sabrina Cho. Your dog is really sweet."

Okay, I thought, so brains aren't everything. Sabrina and I walked along the shoreline at Dog Beach, exchanging phone numbers just as the water was starting to turn my feet a serious shade of blue. When Sally and I got home, I dialed Sabrina's number.

103

"Who dis calling?" The man on the other end of the line sounded a tad angry.

"This is Les Vitek. I met Sabrina on the beach today and she asked me to call."

"She no talk to you. You leave my daughter alone." I was stunned when the dial tone sounded, signaling an end to my first score with the dog magnet.

The next day, Jamie tried to slough it off.

"You've got to give it a chance, Lester." She was flushed and rosy after her lunchtime run. We were sitting in my cubicle, sharing a Subway sandwich. "There are plenty more women out there who are dying to meet you." She bit into the sandwich and cursed when the tomato fell in her lap.

"I'm doomed to bachelorhood," I said glumly, pulling the pickles out of my sandwich and handing them to Jamie. "Besides, that one wasn't the sharpest tool in the shed."

"Relax, Lester. It'll be fine." Jamie downed the pickles and gave me a slap on the shoulder before leaving my cubicle.

The next evening *was* fine. After a quick run near my apartment complex, I saddled up Sally and headed back to Dog Beach. This time, there were a number of women to choose from, all young and delicious and beautiful, and all walking their dogs. I zeroed in on a petite brunette, with wavy hair and jeans slung low on her hips.

"Hi. Nice dog you've got there." She was walking a runty-looking mutt, with sea foam and slobber all over his beard.

"You have a nice dog, too." She looked at me with slightly tilted green eyes and the most beautiful smile I'd ever seen. I was so smitten, I almost released Sally's leash.

"Do you come here a lot?" It turned out that she did. Her name was Tatiana and she was a foreign exchange student from Russia. We swapped phone numbers and as soon as Sally and I got back to my apartment, I dialed Tatiana's number. This time a man didn't answer, and we made a date for Friday night. I was so ecstatic, I dialed Jamie's cell to tell her the good news.

"Hello?" Her voice sounded muffled, and she was sniffling as if she'd been crying.

"Hey, Jamie, it worked. Sally reeled in a good one. She's beautiful and sweet and she's going out with me this Friday."

"Great, I'm really happy for you." Jamie didn't sound convincing.

"What's the matter? Are you catching a cold?"

"Yeah. Something like that." Her voice sounded small and tired. I made excuses to let her go.

At work the next day I stood in Jamie's cubicle gloating about my new prospect.

"I owe it all to you," I said. "If this one works out, I'll make sure you're in the wedding party. Hey, maybe you can be my best man."

Jamie didn't laugh. She didn't look up from her keyboard either, so I knew something was wrong.

"What?" I asked. "Are you all right?"

"Oh, Monica and I are going through some stuff. It's not a big deal." She sniffed as she slid the mouse across the desk pad.

Poor Jamie. I knew she wouldn't want to go over the details; she hated people who did that. But I had to ask. It was part of our routine.

"Want to talk about it?"

"No." She gave me a wan, wet smile.

"You sure?" She nodded her head yes and I put my hand on her shoulder.

"Okay. I'll let you know how the big date goes." I waved goodbye and left her to her work.

My date with Tatiana on Friday began smoothly enough, although I was a little disconcerted when she answered her door with the ugly mutt leashed and ready to go.

"You don't mind if Tolstoy comes along, do you? Tatiana looked at me with those incredible green eyes and I would have said yes to anything.

"Well, I was thinking dinner and a movie, but maybe we can get some take-out and walk on the beach." Improvising was not my strong suit, but I could fake it, on occasion.

"Oh, that would be perfect," she answered as she dragged Tolstoy down the stairs and into my car. I cringed a little when the first blob of slobber hit the leather seat, and then decided to roll with it. We ate fish tacos at Rubio's and spent the evening walking the beach and talking. Tatiana told me about her life in Russia and how she had always dreamt of coming to the United States. She wanted to be a dancer and was hoping to move to LA to try the theater scene once she was through with school. I was certain she liked me. Until I got her home, that is.

"Well, this was fun." My words were more a question than a statement. I leaned against her front door while she fumbled in her backpack for her keys. The mutt was whining and scratching at the door and when Tatiana finally opened it, he fled inside as if he was being chased by coyotes. Tatiana put one foot inside the door and gave me a lukewarm smile.

"It was very nice, this evening, yes?" she said.

"Yes, yes," I answered hoping that she'd keep moving and I could follow her inside. Instead she stepped completely into the apartment and turned back to face me, blocking the doorway with her body.

"Um, I think maybe you should not come in tonight," she said, looking behind her into the apartment as she spoke.

Okay, I thought to myself, I can salvage this. "Would you like to- ?" I was going to ask her if she wanted to go out again sometime, but at that moment, I heard a snort in the room behind her. It would have been all right if it had been an animal snort, but it wasn't. It was distinctly human. And it was male.

"Is there someone there?" I asked trying to peer around her.

"Um, yes, there is something I should tell you," she began, but I stopped her right there. I know a taken female when I see one.

"Ah, I think I get the picture," I said. "Good night, Tatiana."

"Good night, Les. I'm so sorry- " She started to apologize but the snort behind her became a full-sized sniff and then a hawk and spit. Raising my finger to my lips, I turned and walked back to my slobbered-up car. I spewed curses the whole way home.

"God damn it all to hell!" Slamming the steering wheel with my fist, I reached down and cranked up the radio, hoping to relieve the pain by giving myself a splitting headache. "Damn Sally, too. And damn Josh and Jamie for setting me up like the idiot I am!" It was tough to shout over Steve Tyler's screaming rendition of *Janie Got a Gun*, but Aerosmith had nothing on me.

When I got home, my cell phone buzzed in my pocket. I tapped the message app and slumped on the couch. Sally padded over and rested her head in my lap as I read Jamie's text. "Feeling down tonight," it read. "Stop by later? I'll be up."

I leaned my head back on the couch and thought about Jamie. She was a good friend. Heck, she was smart and beautiful and funny, and she deserved to have me rush to her side, even if she had set me up for a second dose of humiliation.

When I got to Jamie's apartment it was eerily quiet. You could usually hear the beats of grunge rock or Jamie's favorite Indian yoga chants, but tonight yielded only the quiet murmur of the neighbors' TV. The door finally opened on the second set of knocks. Jamie's girlfriend, Monica, stood there in t-shirt and pajama bottoms, a huge shiner circling her right eye.

"Hi, I'm Les. What happened to you?" I feared the worse: Jamie had gone off the deep end and whacked her lover.

"Nice to meet you. I'm Monica. Jamie talks about you all the time," she shook my hand firmly and then realized that I was still staring at the bulls-eye above her right cheekbone.

Oh, that." Monica put a hand against the side of her face and gave a weak laugh. "It's a little embarrassing. My kick-boxing instructor caught me in the face yesterday. It looks worse than it feels."

It did look bad. With a sense of déjà vu, I peered around her through the doorway, trying to see if Jamie was inside.

"Are you looking for Jamie?" Monica asked. "She went out with Kristina for a while. I think they needed to talk." Monica looked down at the ground when she said this. A wave of sympathy washed over me. I knew the feeling of being rejected.

"I'm sorry. Tell Jamie I came by." I stood there awkwardly for a moment and then turned to go.

"Hey, wait," Monica said. "You can come in for a while if you want."

Now, if this had been a movie, the music would swell, I would turn around, pause for a strategic second, and then say yes, all romantic and full of hope. But this was Jamie's *girlfriend*. I did turn around, but I had to think about it for a minute. I mean, Monica was pretty, in a petite, spunky kind of way -- glossy black hair, cute smile, big shiner on her right eye. And there was something about her that seemed smart and kind. *More than good enough*. I could hear Jamie's voice in the back of my head. But, I wondered, did lesbians like loser guys who couldn't get dates with straight girls? Who cares, I decided. It was company.

We sat outside on the porch drinking Heinekens. After the third beer, our discussion turned pretty serious.

"Jamie thinks the world of you," Monica said. "I'd say she liked you, if I didn't know her better."

"Jamie's a great girl." My words slurred together, courtesy of the beer. "Don't you think so?"

Monica peeled the label from the bottle in her hand. She seemed to be buying herself a little time before answering.

"Jamie is the most amazing person I've ever met. Maybe too amazing." Monica gazed up at the stars and then looked at me dead on, without flinching. "She doesn't love me, you know."

I don't know what possessed me at that moment. I mean she was Jamie's lover. Guess I was feeling sorry for her and maybe for myself, too. Because what I did next was totally spontaneous. I put my arm around her, kissed her, and told her it was going to be all right. But the incredible thing was, I really meant it. I wanted nothing more at that moment than to make Monica feel better.

What she did was pretty amazing, too, although it may not seem that way to anyone else. She didn't say anything, she just put her head on my shoulder.

"What're you gonna do about the bet?" Jamie sat on the edge of my desk at work. It was November 20, and I was two days away from turning 25.

"Guess I lose," I said, not turning my gaze from the computer.

"Guess again, big guy. Monica wants you to come over for Thanksgiving dinner on Thursday."

I looked up at her and tried to think of something to say. Jamie didn't know that Monica and I were seeing each other. At least I thought she didn't.

"Is that okay with you?" I finally asked.

Jamie paused a moment, presumably to toy with me.

"Well, Kristina's coming over, too." She gave me the full-on Jamie grin. "But here's the bad news; you can't bring Sally. Monica doesn't like dogs."

PORTAL GALLERY

"Put it in the corner with the Sheila Rossi's," Muriel said. She pointed a lumpy finger, its long sharp nail painted port wine red, towards a stack of wrought iron angels near the gallery entrance. "Where's my muffin? Michael was supposed to bring me a nice blueberry muffin this morning."

Michael bustled into the storeroom, corkscrew hair flying in a halo around his head, bearing a pink box that trailed powdered sugar from its corners.

"Here I am. Gertrude's was terrible this morning." He dumped the box on his wife's desk and dipped in a pudgy hand to retrieve a bear claw. "There was only one muffin left. I wanted rugelach, but the bear claws looked too yummy." Michael

114

spoke with a mouth full of pastry and lips coated with sugar crystals. "Have one, Samuel, before you get thin. Muriel, aren't you going to eat anything? I waited twenty five minutes in line to get this for you."

"Yes, yes," Muriel answered, waving her chubby hands at her husband. "Just give me a minute." She moved a stack of invoices and telephone notepads over to the only bare spot on the desk. "Karen! Where did Karen go? I want her to put the Sturman dragonflies in the window."

Karen rushed in, draped from her neck to her feet in black leather, her arms loaded with white cardboard boxes.

"The candleholders are here," she said. "Where do you want them?"

"Let me see one," Muriel said.

Juggling the stack in her arms, Karen handed her a white box and hurried to the back corner to dump the rest of the boxes on top of a pile of paper mache' pigs with cellophane wings.

"Watch the pigs!" Muriel shrieked, as she held up a delicate green glass candleholder in the shape of a water lily. "Ummm, nice. What do you think, Michael?"

"What? Oh, yes, very nice." Michael didn't look up from the pink box, where he was poking around for another bear claw.

"Does anyone want to help me hang the mirrors?" Samuel Portnoy, Muriel and Michael's son, stood at the door of the storeroom, holding a hammer and a box of brads.

"Yes, yes, I'll be right there," Michael said. He popped another piece of pastry in his mouth, and wiped his hands on his jeans before following Samuel through the storeroom door and into the gallery.

"That Oksana woman called again yesterday," Muriel said to Karen, who was pulling wooden clocks shaped like flowers from the top of the storeroom shelf. "I keep telling her that it's a bad time, with the 'Spring Illusions' show opening today and the candle show only a month away."

"What does she want this time?" Karen asked, her voice muffled behind a giant copper wall hanging shaped like a cactus.

"She said she has something special, some reflective thing," Muriel answered. She scribbled into a large black ledger. The numbers for last month actually looked good. "It's always something special with her. Then her stuff gets here and it doesn't sell. I'm tired of warehousing her mediocre art. She should take it downtown to the swap meet or something." Muriel reached into the pink box and pulled out the only muffin.

"Bran," she said. "I told him I wanted blueberry."

"Maybe you should see her one more time," Karen said. "Maybe she's really got something."

"Fat chance," Muriel said, wiping a crumb from the corner of her mouth. "Besides, I've carried too many of her bad ideas already. We deal in whimsy here, not craft store kitsch."

"Well, good luck putting her off," Karen said, as she headed out of the storeroom with an armful of painted watering cans.

"Ummm, hmmm," Muriel mumbled, her mouth full of muffin. The zebra-striped telephone on her desk began to ring.

"Portal Gallery," she gulped into the phone, almost choking on a small piece of pastry that had lodged in her windpipe.

"Ah, my dear Muriel, how are you today?" Oksana Severnaya's voice gushed loudly from the black and white receiver. Muriel held it away from her ear. "I couldn't stop thinking about your spring art show today, and I told myself 'Oksana, how can Muriel open this show without these wonderful pieces. It just isn't possible.' You must see them, Muriel, you absolutely must. When can I bring them over?"

Muriel closed her eyes and pressed her free hand to her forehead. "Oh, Oksana, it's so kind of you to call and offer, but the show opens today and you know how cramped we are for space. Besides, I've got the reporter from *The Tribute* coming this afternoon. I'm afraid today just won't work. Maybe we can get together sometime next week. We'll be much calmer then." Muriel stopped speaking and held her breath, hoping that Oksana would take the hint.

"Oh, but Muriel, this can't wait," Oksana said, her tone serious.

"Why not?" Muriel asked.

"Because these pieces will not be here next week," Oksana answered. "These pieces are one time only items. If you don't take them now, you will never have another chance."

"Why?" Muriel said. "What is it you're trying to sell me this time?'

"Stay right there," Oksana said. "I'll be right over."

Muriel closed her eyes in exasperation as the dial tone buzzed in her ear. She hung up the telephone and stood up, brushing futilely at the crumbs clinging like small aphids to the front of her purple angora sweater.

In the gallery, chaos reigned. Open boxes and piles of Styrofoam peanuts lay strewn in every corner, while the tails of small paper kites that hung from the ceiling bobbed wildly in the breeze from the ceiling fan. Michael and Samuel stood behind the gallery window, a real life Laurel and Hardy display. Samuel wobbled dangerously at the top of a ladder, struggling to hang a daisy-shaped mirror on the wall, while Michael held onto the ladder below him, legs spread-eagled and arms shaking.

"Careful, Samuel," Muriel called out. "We don't want any bad luck."

Samuel turned at the sound of his name and caught himself as the ladder tipped dangerously to one side.

"Leave the boy alone, Muriel," Michael yelled. "You're gonna kill us here."

Muriel shifted her gaze towards the rear of the gallery, where Karen and Marsha were creating a pyramid-shaped display of painted wooden boxes and enameled clay pots.

"What happens when a customer wants the one on the bottom?" Muriel asked.

The two girls looked at her blankly.

"Do you want us to undo it?" Marsha asked.

"That would be a start."

Sighing, Muriel turned to the display counter in the center of the store, and opened the cash register to count the tray. She had gotten through the twenties, when she heard the unmistakable sound of Oksana Severnaya's clicking heels as she clattered into the gallery.

"There you are, Muriel, looking as gorgeous as always," Oksana gushed, knocking over a stand of walking sticks as she tottered to the counter. She was a small woman in her late-seventies, with hair dyed the color of motor oil, and turquoise eye shadow that went all the way up to her eyebrows. Her standard outfit, a swirl of multicolored chiffon scarves over a jacket with a giant rainbow painted on its backside, was accented today with an enormous lizard brooch. In her hands she carried two plastic grocery bags, filled with small, sharp angled objects.

"I have something very special for you," Oksana said in a hushed voice.

"What could be so special that you bring it in a trash bag?" Muriel asked, wishing she had locked the front door.

Oksana leaned over the counter towards Muriel. "These are magic kaleidoscopes," she whispered. "They bring special luck to anyone who looks through them."

"Oh, Oksana, please," Muriel said. "I'm too busy to do this today."

"No, no, no," Oksana said. "You must see them. They really do have magic. The artist who created them says that whoever looks through them can see the future, and whoever passes them by will weep for the past."

"So, if I don't unload this crap for you, my life is doomed, right?"

"Yes, yes," Oksana said, nodding her head vehemently.

"Oksana, do you think I'm an idiot?" Muriel shook her head. "I've got $85,000 worth of inventory sitting on my shelves, I'm opening a new show in twenty-four hours, *The Tribute* is going to be here in twenty minutes, the gallery looks like a herd of Afghan camels has tromped through it, and you want to sell me some magic beans? Please! Go, now, before I ask Michael and Samuel to hang you from the ceiling." Muriel turned back to her cash register.

Oksana's face fell. "Oh, Muriel, you must believe me," she said. "If you don't look at these kaleidoscopes, something terrible will happen."

121

Muriel turned to face her visitor. "Oksana, not today. Not right now. I really don't want to deal with this today." She turned back to the register and began counting twenties again.

Oksana stood quietly for a moment, and then picked up her bags and slowly clicked her tiny feet towards the entrance to the gallery. As she walked out, Karen and Marsha stopped their stacking and turned to watch her go.

"I feel sorry for her," Karen said. "She's just trying to make a buck."

"Trying Muriel's patience is more like it," Marsha answered. She picked up a box and turned back to her work.

That evening, the show opening was crowded. Muriel and Michael mingled among their guests, handed out cups of tea and plates of cookies, and paused for photographs with their showcased artists. When the local television crew arrived, Muriel pointed out the blown glass tree ornaments, the wrought iron garden rack, and the ceramic yard thermometers.

"It's wonderful to see the miracles these artists have wrought with common garden objects," Muriel told the reporter. "When we first opened Portal Gallery ten years ago, it was hard to find artists who were willing to create pieces like this. But we're finding a lot more artists willing to stretch themselves now." As she spoke, she noticed Harold, the homeless man who liked to crash their gallery receptions, circling around the crowd in pursuit of the buffet table.

"Excuse me, please," she said to the cameraman, as she looked around the room in search of her husband or her son. She couldn't locate either of them in the crowd, so she headed toward the food table herself.

"Hello, Harold," she said, coming up behind him. Even standing two feet away, she could smell the strong mildewy odor coming from his unwashed clothes and long, greasy hair. "If you'll wait a minute, I'll find Michael, and he'll fix you some food." Michael would always put together a plate for Harold at these openings, and then lead him quietly out the door.

Harold turned and gazed at Muriel. He had a flushed, reddened face, and dry cracked lips. His eyes looked sunburned and wild, and when he spoke, Muriel could see how raw and pink his gums were, and how there were just a few dark-colored teeth in his mouth.

"I didn't come to eat," he said. "I came to see the kaleidoscopes." When he spoke, Muriel felt a strange sensation come over her. It was as if the room was suddenly empty, and she stood surrounded by a circle of light that illuminated just her and this homeless man. She looked at Harold and waited for him to speak again.

'I want to see the kaleidoscopes," he repeated.

"We don't have any," Muriel said, feeling strangely empty and weird, as if she were in some kind of dream state.

Harold looked confused for a moment, and then lowered his head. When he did, he seemed to break the spell that had come over him and Muriel.

"I've always wanted to see the kaleidoscopes," he mumbled softly, and then stumbled off through the well-dressed crowd and out the gallery door.

Muriel stood still for a moment and then shook herself slightly. Perhaps she was tired, with all the excitement of the opening, she told herself. She spotted Michael in a corner near the front of the gallery and headed through the crowd to stand by her husband.

The next few days, the gallery was unusually busy. Muriel especially enjoyed the properly dressed tourists who came in looking very serious and haughty and then, inevitably, broke into grins. This was the reason she had started Portal Gallery. She loved humor, and thought that life should have more of it.

On the third day of the garden show, a tiny old woman, dressed all in white, tottered up to the counter and looked at Muriel with small bird-like eyes.

"I hear you have the kaleidoscopes," she said. "I came all the way from Phoenix to buy one."

"I'm sorry," Muriel said, "but this is our annual spring show. We don't have any kaleidoscopes to sell."

"Oh, but you must," the old woman said. "They said that you would have them here."

"What? Who said that?" Muriel asked.

"Why the tour guides told us," the woman said. "They said that you were the only gallery in the country that had them."

Muriel was amazed at this piece of information. "Well, I'm so sorry," she said, "but I'm afraid you've been misled."

The old woman looked at her blankly, as if she didn't understand. "But they told us," she said, sounding as if she were going to cry. "It's the reason we came."

Muriel shook her head and then stepped away from the counter, leaving the woman standing there looking at her forlornly. Muriel headed for the back storeroom.

"Michael," she said. "The strangest thing has happened." She explained the woman's request, and how Harold had said the same thing at the Spring Illusions reception. "Do you think they could be looking for Oksana's kaleidoscopes?" she asked.

"It doesn't seem possible," Michael said, "but maybe they're something we should look at. Why don't you call her and see if she can bring them in again."

Muriel tried all afternoon to reach Oksana, but the number she dialed just rang and rang. She searched through old invoices to see if she could find an address for the elderly art dealer, but all that was listed was a post office box. She looked online, but no name came up in the search engines. When she called the post office, the postmaster told her that it was illegal for him to give out Oksana's contact information.

But I must find her, she told herself, and she spent hours writing postcards and letters to Oksana's post office box. When a week had gone by, and there was no reply, she began to feel desperate, and asked Michael what he thought she should do.

"Well, it looks like there's not much we can do," Michael said. "We'll just have to wait for Oksana to call us."

Two to three customers a day now came into the gallery asking for the kaleidoscopes, but Muriel didn't even bother to reply to their questions. Instead, she spent time on the Internet looking up kaleidoscopes and calling toy stores to see if they had anything remotely like what Oksana had described. She combed toy and novelty stores, and ordered all types of kaleidoscopes, in every shape and size, and soon the gallery storeroom was filled with boxes that towered to the ceiling.

"Our books aren't looking so good," Michael said to Muriel one evening. "We've spent last month's receipts on these toys you keep ordering, and our display stock is starting to dwindle. Our creditors are calling, and the artists want to know what's happening with their consignments."

Muriel sat behind her desk, staring bleakly at the pile of papers that littered its surface. She had let Karen and Marsha go last week, and the work they normally did was starting to pile up.

"I just want to see the kaleidoscopes," she said. She looked up at Michael. "Why didn't I look at them when they were here?"

127

Michael shook his head and gazed sadly at his wife. "We may have to close the gallery, Muriel," he said.

Three months later, on a late evening after she and Michael had placed the "Closeout Sale" sign in the gallery window, Muriel was packing up the few remaining items when she heard a soft tapping sound. She looked up and saw Oksana standing at the gallery window, her colorful scarf wrapped around her head. Muriel hurried to the door, and fumbled with the lock to let her friend in, but by the time she got the door open, the street was empty, and no one was in sight. She called out, "Oksana! Oksana!" and looked left and right, but there was no answer.

When she finally turned to go back inside, she noticed a small blue box sitting on the sidewalk below the window. She picked up the box and carried it inside. Her hands shook with excitement as she pried the lid open. At the bottom of the box lay a tiny triangular-shaped kaleidoscope, its sides made of a silvery reflective glass that picked up the prismatic colors thrown by the lights in the room.

Muriel lifted the kaleidoscope towards the light, closed one eye, and peered into the smaller end. Inside she saw a brightly colored cavalcade of diamond shapes that tumbled and converged as she twisted the toy's wide end. As she continued to twist

128

the kaleidoscope, she noticed that the colors and shapes began to merge and blur together.

This is strange, she thought, closing her eyes and giving her head a shake. When she opened her eyes, she saw Samuel standing in a synagogue, in full military dress, his head shaved and his shoulders back. He stood before a rabbi, and a woman in white walked toward him, a bouquet of daisies in her hand. Muriel shook her head again and when she opened her eyes this time she saw Michael, sitting in a small boat, a khaki cap on his head, and a fishing rod across his knee as he baited a hook. In a green field in the background, she could see herself, a heavy-set older woman, holding a small child by the hand and carrying a silver bucket of small, round blueberries.

Michael came up behind her, his breath warm in her ear.

"What is it?" he asked. "What do you see?"

Muriel's hands trembled as she lowered the kaleidoscope. She gazed into her husband's eyes.

"Everything," she said. "I see everything."

She patted Michael's arm, and then reached behind him to close the gallery door.

WEATHERMAN

George Carlyle's family hated him.

Even though he was a popular television weatherman at Station KXRG in San Diego, there were no adoring fans at his house. His wife, Nadine, a Japanese woman who had once been a beauty queen, resented him for saddling her with two children and placing her in the suburbs. She had always felt destined for a classier locale.

"Why can't you get a contract in LA?" she questioned him one morning, while jerkily applying mascara to a kohl-lined eye. "We could live in Brentwood if you worked at KTLA."

His daughters, Karla and Caitlin, chose to ignore him, unless his weather calls were wrong.

"I thought you said it was going to rain, Dad." Caitlin glared at him over her breakfast cereal, her almond-shaped eyes crunched into a squint.

"All my friends say you don't really know anything about the weather. You're just a talking head," Karla added. Blond-haired like George and olive-skinned like her mother, she spooned cereal into her mouth without even looking at him.

His Scripps Ranch neighbors weren't too friendly, either. Dick Mossman would wave half-heartedly at him when he pulled up in the drive in his SUV, but the wife, Clare, wouldn't look him in the eye at all. His few friends from college never called and most of his coworkers at the station avoided him, pretending they were too busy when he asked them to join him at Submarina for lunch. Even his prize pit bull, Max, ignored him, looking up expectantly whenever the door opened and then lying his massive head back down on his soggy pillow once he realized it was George.

He was an easy-going fellow: willing to help whenever the station manager asked him to do some community assignment or a staff member needed assistance. He had brownish-blonde hair, and blue eyes and his build, though slightly pudgy, was distributed evenly enough that he looked sturdy and firm in his two-tone suits during the evening weather broadcasts.

George loved doing the weather broadcasts. When he got to work at four o'clock in the afternoon, he would position himself in front of the Doppler radar system and type in the San Diego location indicators on its keyboard. Although the weather rarely changed—it was usually a temperate seventy degrees in San Diego—George relished the sense of power he derived from being able to predict the days ahead. It made him feel like a kind of benevolent magician who could see into the future and help the people of San Diego prepare for the unexpected, should it ever come.

George always tried to put something interesting or exciting in his evening broadcast, even if the weather was the same day after day, which it often was.

"The Doppler radar is forecasting clear skies and sunny days for San Diego," he predicted in many pre-broadcast announcements. "But a coastal eddy is forming off of Baja California. We'll take a close look at that later in the broadcast."

George felt that by giving his viewers a hint of some impending weather crisis, however remote, he was helping them realize the serendipitous nature of the weather. Even in San Diego where it seemed always the same, the weather could, George thought, blow up on them at any time.

During the eleven o'clock news weather segment, George liked to point toward the teleprompter, his hands underlining the swirling coastal clouds that hung off the Baja Coast.

"You never know, folks," he warned in one broadcast, when the San Diego temperature had been a steady eighty degrees for ten days. "If one of these coastal eddies were to reach our shores, we could have a hint of rain." Here he paused dramatically, looking head-on into the camera. "Even a few showers."

During this particular broadcast, a San Diego State student, who was working at the station as an intern, guffawed loudly enough to be heard on camera. The station manager wanted to fire the student, but George intervened and convinced his boss to give the kid another chance. The weather, George told his station manager, didn't always bring out the best in everyone.

George's boss, Hank Farnsworth, was a short gray-haired man with a bristling five o'clock shadow and a poor sense of humor. One day, when George had been at the station for three years, Farnsworth called him into his office and asked him to shut the door.

"You know your contract is running out next month," he told George after waving him into chair. "I don't know if the owners will renew you."

Nadine, he was sure, would be happy to hear he might be let go; she relished the thought of being able to live in a more upscale city. But George felt a real affinity for San Diego. He liked the sunshine and the beaches and the quiet way the leaves on the palm trees in his backyard swayed in the breeze in the evening. He didn't want to leave Station KXRG, but he knew he couldn't take a salary cut, either. There was no way Nadine would go for that. So he remained quiet while Farnsworth spoke, smiling at him in his bland, friendly way.

"I just wanted to fill you in, George. You know, in case the word comes down next month." Farnsworth gazed at George and ran his hand over his bristly chin.

"Thanks, Mr. Farnsworth," George said, standing up and extending his hand. "If there's anything I can do to prevent this, please let me know."

Farnsworth looked skeptical. "Geez, George, short of working some sort of miracle, I don't know what else you could do. That's the news business in this town. It doesn't ever change."

When George got back to his seat at the Doppler radar station, his stomach felt a little queasy. He almost wished he didn't know the layoff was coming. Now he would have to tell Nadine. He typed in the location numbers for the San Diego coast and waited for the system to boot. As he did, he noticed a slight delay in the results. The radar system, which was usually quick in its response, was hesitating.

NO RESULTS AVAILABLE AT THIS TIME.

George stared at the screen. The system had never given this reading before. He typed in the coordinates a second time and waited, noticing again a slight hesitation in the system before the same screen message came up.

NO RESULTS AVAILABLE AT THIS TIME.

George stared, this time in disbelief. He wasn't familiar with this error message. After searching without success for the system manual, he tried typing in some other coordinates. The screen gave the same response, over and over. George finally slumped back in his chair, defeated. Well, it's a good thing we're in San Diego, he thought, since the weather is always the same anyway. He headed over to the teleprompter computer to prepare for the evening news segment.

That night he gave the weather straight, with no warnings, no swirling coastal eddy clouds or arrows pointing to high winds in the north, no undulating ribbons of white showing the jet stream. Just the weather, as it had always been.

"Tomorrow will be a typical June day in San Diego," he said. "Coastal temperatures in the mid-seventies and inland temperatures in the low to mid-eighties. This is George Carlyle, wishing you a wonderful and safe tomorrow." George signed off with his friendly smile.

The next morning, when he opened the door to get his newspaper, he was met by a cold bristling wind that blew his hair back and caused his bathrobe to flap wildly around him. He held his hand up to his eyes and squinted at the front lawn, which was covered with a light coating of frost, glistening and white on the green carpet of grass. George stumbled down the front walkway, his slippers skidding on a thin sheet of ice. He picked up his newspaper, which had not been wrapped in plastic. It dripped gray ink, a sodden mass of black pulp. The ominous slate-colored sky darkened as he gazed up at it. George walked gingerly back into the house and called Nadine and the girls to come look outside.

"Jesus Christ," Nadine said, pulling her green silk kimono tightly around her thin chest. "Where did this come from?"

"Great, Dad. Another accurate forecast from the San Diego weatherman." Krista sneered.

136

"I want to play in the snow!" Caitlin said, pulling on her mother's kimono.

"That's not snow, honey, its frost." But just as George spoke, a few light flakes of snow drifted out of the sky and landed softly on the pavement outside the front door. "Unbelievable." George stared.

George drove to the station carefully that afternoon, keeping his lights on and inching forward through the light flurries that dusted the roads of the city. When George got to work, the entire newsroom was buzzing. Everyone crowded around the table at the afternoon staff meeting, waiting for Farnsworth to enter the room.

"Where's Carlyle?" Farnsworth stuck his head in the staff room door and motioned for George to follow him outside. "What's going on, George? The whole city's gone crazy."

"I don't know how to explain it," George said. "The Doppler radar shows an unexpected cold front that just swooped in on us. It seems to have come out of nowhere."

"Well, find out where it came from. And tell Henricks he's off the anchor desk. You're leading off at six o'clock."

"I'll see what I can do," George mumbled to himself, as if he hadn't heard his boss at all. "I'll check the radar; maybe the weather will change tomorrow."

"Hell, let's hope not," Farnsworth said, "We finally have some real news in this city."

That evening, the entire population of San Diego tuned into Station KXRG's six o'clock news. Even George's family watched from the theater-sized television in their living room.

"Unbelievable," Nadine muttered when she saw her husband giving the lead story.

"Why is Daddy's suit all bunched up?" Krista asked. George hadn't unbuttoned his suit jacket when he sat down at the news desk, which made his collar sit unnaturally high around his ears.

"We've had an unexpected cold front here in San Diego." George spoke from the news desk, where he'd never sat before. "Frigid air from the north has brought low pressure and high winds to coastal and inland areas in the County. Lindbergh Field reports one-to-two inches of snow in the last hour and folks in Julian are digging out from under thirteen inches of snow that fell in the mountains this afternoon." George wiped the sweat from his hands on his suit pants underneath the anchor desk. "I'll have more for you on this unexpected weather front when we return after these brief announcements."

The newsroom staff crowded around him during the commercial break, handing him text copy and helping to straighten out his suit. One of the interns, a dark-haired college student from UCSD, slapped him on the back and told him he was doing a good job. George blinked at her in surprise.

For the next three days, the winter storm blew snow into San Diego. George got to the newsroom at noon each day, after scraping his SUV's windshield with a credit card and driving at a crawl through icy streets. He checked the Doppler radar, waiting until it sluggishly responded, the precipitation intensity showing up as a jerky blotch of moving red pixels on the screen. George anchored the news each night, giving the latest update on the storm, the number of inches of snow piling in front of houses, the severity of the accidents occurring on San Diego freeways. Newspaper and magazine reporters called George to interview him. The mayor came by to inspect the Doppler radar equipment. The fire department invited him to do a photo shoot near Warner Springs where an extra heavy pile of snow had forced a tree, like an enormous javelin, into the roof of a local store.

Through all the commotion, George barely noticed that the newsroom staff had begun to acknowledge him. The receptionists at the front desk greeted him kindly. The anchors waved to him on their way into their offices, and the interns brought him lattes from Starbuck's when they made their afternoon coffee runs.

George didn't notice that his family was acting differently, too. He was so busy with the news that he hardly saw them at all, staying late at the newsroom to answer calls from the national weather service, leaving early to help direct segments being filmed by The Weather Channel.

One morning, as he was putting on ski gloves before heading out the door, Caitlin stumbled down the stairs in her pajamas. She held her favorite toy, a floppy stuffed rabbit that was once white, but was now covered in a gray stubble of pilled fur.

"Are you going to the snow, Daddy?" she asked, twisting a strand of tousled hair around one stubby finger.

"No, honey, Daddy's going to work." George forced himself to stop a moment, his hand on the door.

"Can I go with you?"

"No, Caitlin. It's a school day."

"Are you going to stop the weather?" Caitlin gazed at him, her almond-shaped eyes wide and serious.

George pulled on the knob and opened the door a crack, letting in a gust of icy air.

"No, Daddy can't stop the weather. Besides, I kind of like it," he said before giving her a kiss on the forehead and stepping out into the cold.

At eleven o'clock that morning, George's desk phone rang. He answered without looking up from the NOAA reports he was screening.

"I thought we might have lunch today." The voice was Nadine's, but George almost didn't recognize it, since she rarely called him at the station. They agreed to meet at the Fish Market, an upscale restaurant overlooking San Diego harbor.

"The girls and I hardly see you these days." Nadine pouted and raised a shoulder coyly as she stirred her Bloody Mary with a celery stalk. They were seated on the second floor of the restaurant, near a window. Nadine was wearing a red silk blouse that he hadn't seen before.

"We're just so busy at the station. No one's ever seen weather like this. It's big news." They both gazed out at the bay, the water charcoal-colored and glassy under a dark sky. George glanced at his watch. The service was slow and he wanted to get back to the newsroom.

"Maybe we can get away this weekend, go up to the mountains? The girls would love to stay in a cabin." Nadine looked at George expectantly, as if she were waiting for the friendly smile, the innocuous George grin.

"Sure, we could do that," George answered vaguely as he signaled the waiter for the check.

When he got back to the newsroom, after almost skidding into another car in the parking lot, there were a pile of pink phone message slips on his desk and Farnsworth was waiting outside his door.

"Something's happening in the weather," Farnsworth said. "We got word that the storm might be breaking."

George hurried over to the Doppler station and fed in the San Diego coordinates. The machine responded quickly this time, showing a greenish orange patch of pixels over the inland valley.

"It's rain," he said. "The snow has turned to rain." George felt strangely light-headed, as if he was going to be dizzy. He reached for a chair and sat down.

"Too bad," Farnsworth said. "We had some decent ratings while it lasted."

In the days that followed, the storm slowly abated. Snow flurries dissolved into freezing rain and then into light showers and occasional spots of drizzle. George was relegated to his former weather segment, at the end of the eleven o'clock news program. As the weather subsided into its normal spring pattern of coastal gloom, George no longer came in early to tune into the Doppler radar and he kept his forecasts to the weather at hand, with no hints of possible changes or impending crises.

At home, his children ran up to greet him when he walked in the door, passing him the main course at dinner first before helping themselves. His coworkers invited him out to lunch and the neighbors, even Clare Mossman, greeted him openly each day, waving at him from behind the windshield of her minivan. Nadine came by the office once a week to take him shopping or out to lunch, but George was untouched by all of it. The weather had become a traitor to him. By proving itself to be capricious and newsworthy, the recent storm had rendered George's predictions small and meaningless. It had made him truly insignificant.

Two months after the snowstorm, when San Diego was enjoying its usual eighty- degree mid-August weather, George stood across from Farnsworth's desk.

"I can't believe you're doing this," Farnsworth said. "The station renewed your contract. Do you realize how infrequently that happens in this town?" He leaned back into his desk chair, his hand rubbing at the three-day growth of hair on his chin.

George put his hand on the Emmy statuette that Farnsworth kept on the desk. He felt the tip of the statue's wings, ran his finger over its golden back.

"I'm sorry, but I can't do this anymore. The weather, I mean. It just isn't the same." George shook his head. "It just isn't the same," he repeated softly.

"Well, good luck to you." The two men shook hands and George shuffled to his office to gather his personal items. As he headed toward the station door, a small cardboard box in his hands, he heard a voice call his name.

"Mr. Carlyle!" It was the San Diego State student, the one who had laughed at him during his broadcast. The kid ran toward him now, waving a newspaper in his hand. "You forgot this, sir," he said.

George juggled the box so that he could take the paper with one hand. "Thanks," he said. When he got outside the door, he loaded the box into the SUV and then stopped to look at the newspaper. It was the front page of the *San Diego Union-Tribune*, dated June 6, 2002. "Freak Snowstorm Hits San Diego," the headline read. Below it was a photograph of a man trying to pull open an office door as the winds blew against him, whipping his coat away from his big frame. George saw that the man in the photograph was himself, heading into the newsroom office the

144

day the storm broke. *"Channel KXRG weatherman George Carlyle struggles to enter the news station during a record breaking snowstorm that hit the city this morning,"* the caption read.

George smiled at the photograph. Then, taking in a big breath of warm summer air, he tossed the paper into the backseat of his car and drove away.

YOU ARE MY FATHER

Y ou hand me a brown bottle of San Miguel beer.

"Want a drink, Julio? Sip it slowly. There you go."

I taste the cool, fizzy liquid on my tongue and choke as I swallow, making a face at the bitterness of it. My reaction is swift for a boy of ten. You take the bottle from my hand and laugh, telling me that I'll learn to like it someday. You lift the beer to your lips and lean your head back to drink. Your hair is black and curly, and the skin on your forearm is the same golden color as mine. We sit on the back porch in cutoff jeans and T-shirts, the Los Angeles weather a warm seventy-five degrees. It is two days before Christmas.

You set the bottle down on the back porch and approach the lawnmower, leaning forward to yank the greasy ignition cord in one smooth motion. The mower coughs and then shifts into a deep, grinding roar. I watch you, your eyebrows knit together as you push the mower in neat stripes across the thick dry grass in our backyard. Your muscles ripple underneath your T-shirt and the sweat beads up on your neck. I want to be just like you: tall, strong, afraid of nothing.

Inside the house, my mother sets a pot of water on the stove, then adds beans, salt, and a small bit of lard. Her hair is long, black, and shiny, and she wears small gold hoops in her ears. As she stirs the pot, she hums a Mexican love song; a tune she learned as a girl in her native village of Oaxaca. She is small and brown-skinned, and when I was younger, her eyes would dance with laughter. She smiles when we walk into the kitchen, then stiffens when you stand behind her at the stove. You place your hand on her back, but she does not move. As you walk away, she resumes her stirring, humming a little softer now.

I watch my mother while she cooks and wait until she turns away before reaching down to snatch two small pinto beans that have fallen on the floor. I quickly place them in my pocket. When Mama and I go to the grocery store this afternoon, I know I'll get

147

more. In the produce section, there's a large, tan barrel filled with beans. I like to wait until Mama isn't looking and then plunge my hands into the barrel, pretending the smooth, hard beans are jewels, and I am reaching into a pirate's treasure. If no one is looking, I stash a few in my pocket. Later, when I get home and the afternoon sun has cooled, I plant them alongside the others in the soft, dark earth that lines our back fence.

"We're lucky to have a house with such a big yard," you tell me at the dinner table. "Where I grew up, there were no houses with yards. We lived in shacks with no toilets or running water. We played baseball with balls made of rags and sticks for bats."

My two older sisters, Lupe and Carmen, roll their eyes while you talk. They are both in junior high and like to pretend that everything you say is stupid. They are not called "beaner" and "beanpole" like I am at school. The high school boys like their long hair and golden skin. When you are home, the boys hang out on the sidewalk down the street, knitted caps pulled low across their foreheads, their hands thrust into the pockets of their baggy jeans. If you are gone, they lean against their cars in front of our house, playing cards and waiting for my sisters to come out.

"I remember when we lived in Tijuana," Lupe, the fourteen-year-old, says.

"How can you remember if you were only two?" Carmen, the twelve-year-old, asks her.

"Because I'm smarter than you are," Lupe says, pushing her long dark hair behind her shoulder. "I remember the chickens in the dirt behind our house. One of them tried to bite me." She leans over her plate, a dreamy look in her eyes. "I remember the car Uncle Tito rented to bring us here. It was green and white and had a back window that wouldn't roll up."

"Jacinta, come sit down," you yell to Mama, who is in the kitchen. "We're almost through eating."

"*Si, si,* Diego." Mama appears, carrying more tortillas and another beer for you.

"What time is everyone coming tomorrow?" you ask.

"Two o'clock," Mama answers, taking a seat at the table next to you.

Tomorrow is Christmas Eve and all of our relatives who live near us will be here.

"I have to go down to the docks in the morning," you say, taking a hard drink of your beer.

"They're unloading the day before Christmas?" Mama asks.

149

"Only for a little while. I have some business to take care of."

Everyone looks down at the table when you say this, except me. I don't understand the silence. I have gone to the docks with you and seen your crews unloading the crates: boxes of red grapes from Chile, green bunches of bananas from Ecuador, brown burlap sacks of coffee from Panama. I ask if I can go with you.

"No, Julio, I have too much work to do."

I lower my head. You sit for a moment, thinking, and then say, "Okay, why not?" I jump up from the table and hug you. My sisters roll their eyes again.

The next morning we leave early, while the sky is gray and overcast. As we drive on the freeway, I lean my head against the window and count the palm trees that flash by along the city skyline. Mama has made burritos to take with us for breakfast. Mine feels warm and soft in my hand. We eat in silence.

When we get to the docks, you stop the car outside the chain-link fence where the workers stand in their dirty jeans and worn, gray jackets. You park the car and tell me to stay inside. I roll down the window and breathe in the salt air as I listen to the seagulls' cries overhead. The boats rock slowly on the water, making rough scraping sounds as they bump against the docks. You stand huddled with the workers, talking to them in rapid Spanish that I cannot quite hear. They nod their heads, and then you shake hands with two of them, small men with straw cowboy hats.

When you get back in the car, you lean toward me and place your hand on my head.

"See those men, Julio? They don't have union cards, so they can't come inside. But they are good men. Very good men."

We drive inside the gate and park by the docks. A big red-faced man in blue overalls and a thick jacket comes over and shakes your hand.

"Velasquez," he says. "You brought your boy with you?"

"You remember Julio," you say, placing a proud hand on my shoulder. "Julio, this is our foreman, Senor Newman."

I shake his hand, which feels warm and dry.

"Nice to see you," he says. He pulls you by the shoulder to the side of the dock and lowers his voice.

"Your shipment is in. Can you take it?"

"*Si, si*," you answer. "Tito is coming to pick it up."

Senor Newman looks behind him quickly and then turns back to you.

"Ten o'clock," he says.

"*Si*," you answer again.

I sit on a pile of burlap bags while small dark men unload wooden crates. You sit up high in a metal car, operating an iron forklift that reaches under the crates and stacks them neatly into rows along the far docks. I lean back on the scratchy sacks, feeling the sun on my face as it breaks through the clouds. I am almost asleep when a whistle blows, and I hear someone shout my name.

"Julio!" It is Uncle Tito, standing next to you grinning, the sun reflecting off the front of his big dark sunglasses.

"*Hola, tio*." I wave from my pile of sacks and watch as the two of you talk on the edge of the dock, looking like twins with your matching heads of dark curly hair. Uncle Tito is dressed in white pants and a leather jacket, a large gold watch on his wrist. He slaps you on the back and walks toward the parking lot. You call over to where I'm sitting.

"Stay right there, Julio. I'll be back in a few minutes." You follow Uncle Tito.

On the docks, it's suddenly quiet as the workers take their morning break. I lay back on the rough brown sacks, my eyes closed, thinking of Santa and the presents that will be under the Christmas tree tomorrow morning. I am comfortable and happy until I realize I have to pee.

I know that the portable toilets are at the back of the loading dock, near where we parked, and I stumble along, following the exit signs. When I get to the toilets, I fling open the door and step inside, holding my breath at the smell. I try not to look down at the big dark hole. Once I'm back outside, I let my breath blow out, taking in a deep gulp of clean salt air. It is only after I close the door that I notice Uncle Tito and three of the Mexican workers from outside the gate. They are gathered by his car, a big silver Cadillac, placing blocks wrapped in blue plastic in the trunk. Uncle Tito doesn't see me when I duck behind the toilet. He is standing guard, looking left and right, holding a small pistol in his hand.

"*Apurate*. Hurry," he tells the workers. I watch as they stack the blue blocks under the floor of the trunk. The workers place the last ones inside and then lower the floor mat over them. They slam the trunk shut and walk away. Uncle Tito puts the gun in his belt under his jacket and gets in the car. He starts it up and backs out of the lot. As he turns down the drive, I notice you and the workers. They are standing around you, holding out their hands as you pay them.

I step around the toilet to head back to the docks, but not before you look up and see me standing there.

The seagulls cry, flapping their wings and spinning in circles overhead. I walk back to the docks and sit on my pile of burlap sacks. I am hungry, and I want to go home.

At our house, the party is loud and crowded. Someone has turned on the Christmas lights and they glow weakly in the late afternoon sunlight: red, green, white, blue and then red again. Along the front walkway, my sisters have set out the brown paper bags, each filled with sand and one candle. We will light them tonight at midnight. Inside the house, *tipico* music echoes through all the rooms and rich smells fill the air: tamales, chile rellaenos, and roasted meat, a goat's head that is still cooking in the oven. My aunt, Rosario, hugs me tightly to her chest and then releases me, wiping at my cheeks to remove the lipstick she always leaves there. In the living room, my mother and her other sisters—Renata, Maria, and Socorro—sit in a circle cracking roasted pumpkin seeds in their teeth and sipping tequila from shot glasses. They wave their hands, earrings dangling and gold-rimmed teeth flashing when they tilt their heads back and laugh.

I go outside the house to the backyard, where you and my uncles—Miguel, Hector, Tito, Enrique—stand in the grass, drinking beer and talking. I squat near the corner of the fence and check my bean sprouts. Two of them are just breaking through the earth, their waxy green heads bent low to the ground, the dirt still clinging to the tender shoots.

"What you got there, Julio?" It is Uncle Tito, weaving slightly on unsteady feet.

"Some plantings. Beans," I answer.

"Going to be a farmer, eh?" He shakes his head and shrugs. "Hey, better a farmer than a dope dealer, right Diego?"

You look over at him and nod, waving your beer. After watching Uncle Tito for a moment, you break away from the group to join us.

"What are you doing?" You speak to Tito in a low voice.

"Nothing. I'm not doing anything. I was just telling Julio here that he's better off being a farmer." Uncle Tito backs away, smiling weakly at you. "Everyone should be a farmer."

He stumbles over to my sister, Lupe, who is standing with two of our cousins, Elena and Antonio, near the back door. Uncle Tito puts his arm around

155

Lupe's shoulders and laughs loudly. You watch him for a moment and then rejoin the men who are standing on the grass. Uncle Tito and Lupe lean forward and almost fall onto the porch, my sister raising her hands to steady him. I pat the soft earth and go back into the house.

In the kitchen, my younger cousins are sitting in a circle playing marbles. They reach into battered coffee cans and roll the glass balls on the linoleum floor, shouting excitedly at each other.

"Hey, no steelies!"

"No dropsies either, *cabrone*!"

My cousin, Eduardo, waves to me.

"Julio, come play."

I squat outside the ring of boys and dip my hand into a red Folgers can, feeling among the common cat's eyes until I find a smooth blue and yellow agate.

"You need a one-inch for a shooter," Eduardo says and hands me a large yellow-green cat's eye. I put the marble against my knuckle and line it up with two peewees in the center of the floor. I hit the first one and everyone cheers. As the marbles roll under the kitchen table, I hear a scream. We stop our game and run into the family room. Lupe is standing near the door holding her blouse in front of her, tears running down her face, her hair no longer sleek and smooth. You clutch Uncle Tito by the shirt collar and push him towards the back door. The aunts and uncles crowd behind you as you stumble onto the back porch. Uncle Tito pleads with you.

"It was nothing, Diego. I swear, I did nothing."

You drag Uncle Tito down the porch and across the lawn and slam him against the fence. The entire family is outside, watching as you swing your fist back and hit him across the face. He reels back, the thin wooden fence buckling with a sharp crack. Uncle Tito puts his hands up, palms facing you.

"No, Diego, no. Please. No," he whispers.

You pull back and hit him again, your knuckles making a hard, smacking sound when they connect with his cheek. My uncles gather around you, trying to pull your arms back and separate you from Uncle Tito, but you shake yourself free. Mama and Lupe are standing at the back door now, my sister sniffling and Mama holding her, crying. I wrap my arms around my stomach and watch as you beat my uncle, beat him again and again. It hurts so much to watch that I double over and fall to the ground, my knees sinking in the soft earth, my face wet with tears. When they finally pull you off of Tito, he is limp and bloody and struggling to stand up.

157

You wheel around in the grass, head hanging, chest heaving and look at no one as you stalk past my sister and mother into the house. The rest of the family crowds around Uncle Tito, leaving me kneeling alone on the ground. It is then that I notice my bean plants, crushed and bent flat into the dark earth. I breathe out slowly and try to come to my feet, but the ground feels like water, and the sky above me starts to swirl in a slow, spinning motion.

I let myself drown.

When I wake up, I am lying on my bed in my room. You sit next to me in the dark, your chin in your hands, thinking.

"Papa," I say.

You turn to me and put your hand on my cheek.

"Feeling better, Julio?"

"*Si.*"

"How about a sip of water?" you ask.

I nod.

You lift the glass to my lips and the water tastes cool. I drink all of it.

You put the glass on the nightstand and turn back to look at me. I can see your eyes in the dark, shining and sorrowful like the picture of Jesus on the wall in our living room. The house is quiet, the crickets chirping outside my window.

"Where is everyone?" I ask.

"They all went home."

"Uncle Tito?"

"He's gone, too." You pause and lower your head. I can barely hear your voice. "I'm sorry, Julio," you whisper.

I want to tell you it's okay, that I know Uncle Tito will be all right, that Santa will come tomorrow, and we will celebrate Christmas like always, my sisters trying on their new jewelry, Mama smiling over the breakfast table. But I can't find the words, so I remain silent, fingering the loose threads on the edge of my blanket.

You rub your hands on the back of your neck and then stand up and walk out of the room.

I close my eyes and try to picture the presents under the Christmas tree tomorrow morning. Instead, I see the boats at the harbor, lined up one by one on the dock, their noses bobbing up and down. Above my head the seagulls wheel and turn, and I am flying right behind them, ascending higher and higher into the warm embrace of the clouds.

www.ingramcontent.com/pod-product-compliance
Lightning Source LLC
Chambersburg PA
CBHW071937170626
46813CB00005B/1768